Richy Knight

Searching for Magic

Book Two

Wriiten and Illustrated by

Galina Evangelista

Empire Publishing

www.empirebookpublishing.com

Table of Contents

Richy Knight

The Magic Book

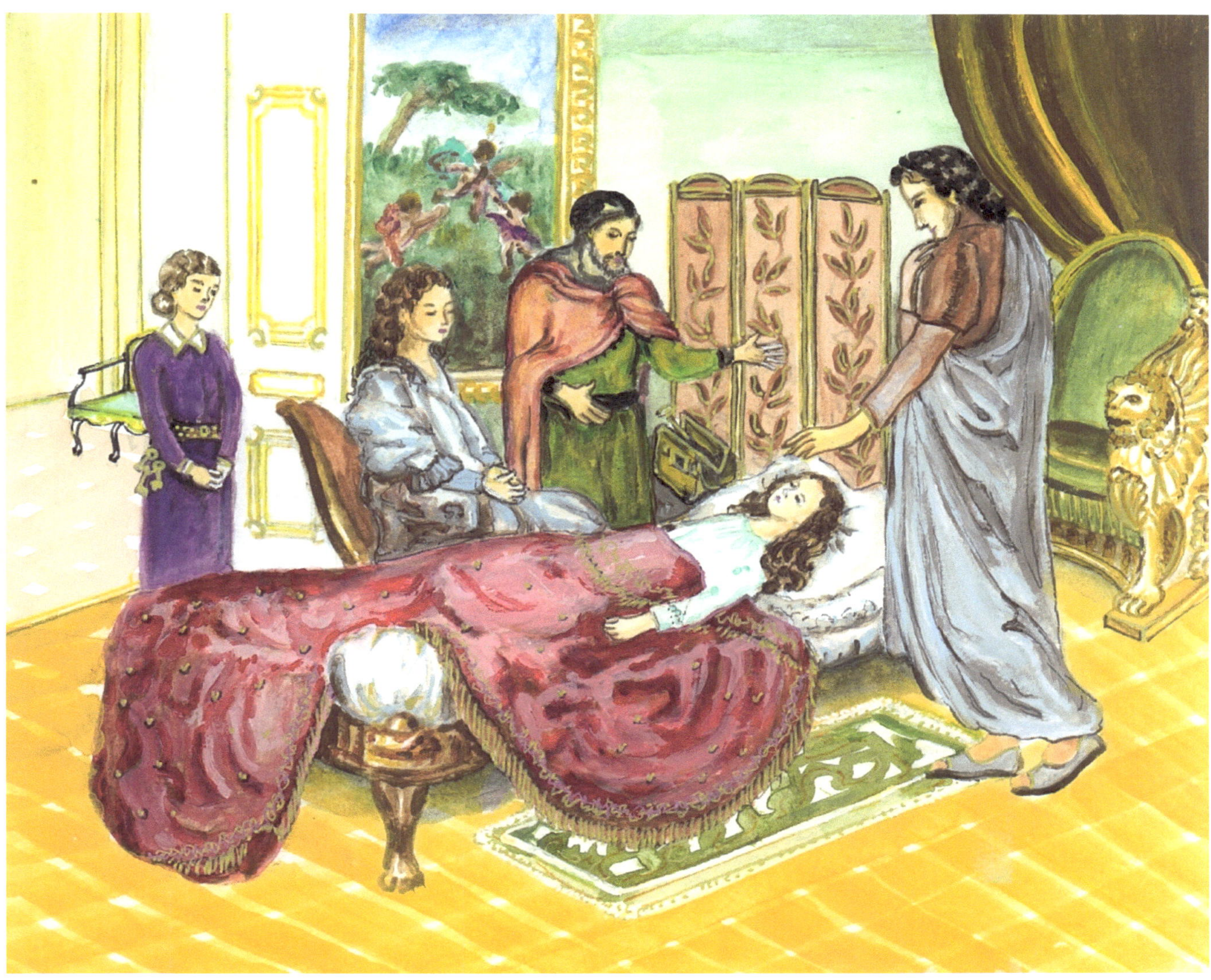

Welcome, Doctor, I've been waiting to bring you to Magi's bed. This way, please," Miss O'Connor nervously running her fingers through the keys dangled from her belt, led the doctor to the staircase.

"How long has it been since it happened?"

"Eleven days have passed, Doctor. We all hope that you can wake her up."

They walked upstairs to Magi's room. Apollonius was standing next to the bed with his head down. Ofelia was sitting and holding Magi's lifeless hand. She got up to give the doctor access to his little patient who was lying motionless on her back. He pulled out a tube from his leather case and put it over Magi's heart.

"She is breathing, and this is a good sign."

On the other side of the city of Sibul, in his shabby old castle, Crowell had a meeting with two ghost-spies.

The same night when the other ghosts invaded the castle of Apollonius, two ghost-spies had a different assignment to find the hidden door. For a long time, Crowell was trying to find that passageway to the secret place. The ghost-spies thought they found it under the staircase. They tried to enter, but it was too solid for them to filter through. At a meeting, they explained their difficulties to their black magic master.

"Yes, we have a problem," Crowell was scratching his bald head. His bulging cross-eyed eyes could not only scare people but ghosts as well. The two spies moved their chairs closer and pressed against each other in fear.

"It's taking too long to get the book," Crowell was talking to himself. "And I did so much work already to distract everyone, like sending the black crows and ghosts, and still no result."

"You can go now. I have no use for you - go, go," he waved his hand, sending them away. "Wait," he changed his mind, "Send me my pupils Burak and Gamut; I have a serious job for them."

His two students were dragging their legs because they were extremely lazy. There was constant quarreling between them, and Burak felt that he has some priority over Gamut, and was always pushing him to do the job he supposed to do. But he was a sheep in front of his master.

They walked into the gloomy room with narrow windows. Water was leaking from the walls and pieces of drywall fell on the stone floor. It was Crowell's crown room with his portrait on the wall behind his armchair. The air in the room smelled like a dead fish because the skeleton of a stinky herring, for some unknown reason, was hanging on a rope over the long old table in the center of the empty room.

"Sit down," Crowell said to them, pointing his skeleton looking hand with red joints to two chairs with only three legs. There was not much left of the seats because the cushions were eaten by moths and through the holes, they could see the floor. Both of them sank into the chairs, making them look smaller than they actually were. They both struggle to balance themselves on three-legged chairs not to fall.

Crowell looked at them angrily, crushing a bag with his foot while he coughed to clear his throat. Standing high over them, the master said with a wheezy voice, "You've lived long enough under my roof and so far have done nothing useful." It was not clear who he is looking at because both pupils in his cross-eyes were angled toward his nose.

"But we are only students, master Crowell," Burak said in small voice.

"Time came for you to grow up," he barked at them and thought to himself," Two wasteful creatures."

"What I'm going to tell you is the highest secrets of all times," Crowell lean on the table to get closer to their faces. "If anyone finds out about it, I will know that you gave out the secret. The penalty for betraying my trust is death; a horrible, painful death," his eyes almost fall out of their sockets. He stood up straight, jerked his bald head like he was throwing back his imaginative hair and continued, "I already did half of the job to put Apollonius's daughter to sleep. The spell that I taught you in class works, and she is sleeping. And only the secret, which is written in the magic book, can wake her up."

He walked around, touching the backs of the chairs on which his pupils were sitting, and that gave them goosebumps.

"This book has passed through many generations of the Apollonius family. It is forbidden not only read the book but even to touch it. I know Apollonius will do anything to save his daughter, even to break the law."

Both creatures were blinking with their eyes, being overwhelmed by the trust of their master.

"The book is in the castle of Apollonius," Crowell continued, and his voice made a whistle. "It's hidden in a secret place and very well protected. You have to find it and bring it to me."

"But Master."

"I know what you want to say, and it's up to you how you get inside the castle. But when you are in, watch Apollonius when he goes to the door under the staircase. Follow him and wait until you see him with the book in his hands and then act fast and take it from him."

Both pitiful creatures looked at each other; now they have to prove to their master that they are worthy.

Another day passed, and Magi didn't wake up. After the doctor's visit, Apollonius knew that it's all Crowell's doing, "He put a spell on her to sleep forever unless I get the book and find the antidote to his spell." Apollonius couldn't find peace with himself. The only way to wake her up is to break the law of centuries.

"I have to do it, I don't have a choice," he said to himself, looking at his lifeless little daughter.

Burak and Gamut didn't waste any time and were already hanging around the Apollonius castle, looking for an opportunity to sneak in.

"The dog," Gamut noticed a dog lying on the grass under a tree. "We can try the spell on him that we learned last week."

"It will be hard not knowing his name."

"Nonsense, it will work," Burak muttered, "We just need to get closer to him."

The gravel gave crunchy sounds under their feet, waking Gasper up. His ears honed in on the sound, but it could be anything, and he put his head back on his feet and closed his eyes.

Behind the bush, Burak was rubbing his hands with his palms, turned to Gasper, and started his spell, "Abracatu- du- radimen separrr." He threw his hands toward Gaspar.

Gaspar raised his head, held it still for a few seconds, and then his head dropped on his paws.

"It works," Gamut exclaimed, rubbing his hands, "We are not that bad of students as master Crowell says about us."

They tested to see if the spell worked by throwing a small stone in Gaspar's direction, but he didn't react.

"He is sleeping, let's go," Burak pushed Gamut. "You carry him."

"He is heavy," Gamut picked up Gaspar from the ground, "He must have a good life here and gets more food than the two of us at Crowell's'."

Seeing that Gamut is struggling to pick up the heavy dog, he commanded, "You take the back, and I will carry his front with the head."

They brought Gaspar closer to the door, and Gamut knocked with the bronze ring on the door. Miss O'Connor happened to be near the door, and she opened it.

"Is it your dog, Mam?"

"Oh, what's wrong with Gaspar?" said Miss O'Connor, surprised to see the motionless pet.

"We found him outside of your property, lying on the road. Looks like that he needs help."

"Thank you for bringing him," Miss O'Connor said in a warm but troubled voice. "Please bring him here, next to the kitchen," she pointed, "there is his place."

They put the dog on his mattress.

"I'll walk you out, thank you again."

"It's alright, Mam, we can find the way to the door. Take care of your dog," they both said at the same time.

Miss O'Connor went to the kitchen to get a piece of meat to make Gasper feel better, and Burak and Gamut hid behind the curtain.

"Ha, ha," Gamut giggled, "She bought it."

"Shoosh, stay still," Burak barked angrily. "If somebody notices the curtain moving, our plan will be doomed to failure."

They stood silently behind the curtain for hours not able to find a better place to hide because every time they attempted to get out, somebody walked into the hall.

"I'm going to faint if I have to stand on my feet longer," Gamut complained.

"Stop it, Stupid," Burak growled at his weak partner. "Any more complaints and I will push you out; then we will see what will happen to you."

Finally, movement in the castle slowed down, and it was dark enough to find the right place to wait for Apollonius to go into the secret door under the staircase. The music room was the most suitable place. From there they could see the secret door.

"Ewe," it's stinky here. It smells like how coffins smell. What are they keeping here?" Gamut fastidiously wrinkled his nose.

"There he is," Burak warned Gamut to be ready.

With oil lamp in his hand, Apollonius was slowly walking down the stairs. He got to the secret door, reached into his pocket, and pulled out a key to unlock the door.

Both intruders were watching for the right moment to follow him.

"Why he is standing in front of the open door and not going inside?" Gamut was wondering.

"Shhh, as soon he goes in, I'll run to grab the door before it can slam shut, and you rush to get inside. I will follow you. Whatever happens, don't make any sounds, clear?"

"Uh huh," agreed Gamut.

The next moment, Burak watched Apollonius disappear behind the doorway. He dashed out of his hiding place and grabbed the handle on the door.

Gamut stormed into the dark doorway, and Burak followed him.

Instead of a solid floor, they were on some sort of gutter, sliding down at an incredible speed. "Smack," Gamut's body made a crashing sound, smashing against the stone floor.

"Smack," Burak landed with a muffled sound landing on Gamut.

They both opened their mouths to scream but didn't dare to make any sound.

"I think I broke my le..,"

"Hlup," Burak slapped Gamut with all his power.

"Shut up, Stupid." He mumbled through his teeth.

They sat on the floor in complete darkness. There was no sign of Apollonius or any life around them.

"Now, what?" Gamut said in a whiny voice. "We can't even get out of here because there are no stairs to climb."

"Shut up, I said," Burak snapped him again.

"I see light over there,"

"Shhh, he is coming, I see him."

There was light to the left of them a minute ago, but it disappeared along with Apollonius.

"We have to move from here. Get up," Burak commanded.

"I can't, my leg is broken," Gamut went into tears.

Burak went berserk. He collected all swearwords and damnations he learned through his life and came down on Gamut with them.

"This is your fault, you told me to follow him," Gamut was crying.

"My fault, you wanted to learn black magic. I didn't drag you to Crowell's doorstep."

That was the truth and Gamut couldn't say anything in his defense. They couldn't say how long they already were sitting at the spot where they crashed, but they were sitting in total darkness and had no place to go.

High up in the castle, Apollonius was standing alone in front of his motionless little daughter in silence with his eyes closed. He was waiting for the waxing moon and the time of a flowing tide.

The ancient Greek philosopher Aristotle believed that no living creature can die except at ebb tide. The thought came to his mind.

Crowell made his spell when the waning moon was in the sky. "There is a waning moon tonight, and it is the right time for black magic," he thought.

Magic is nature, and only nature can create magic. For a long time, he stood next to the bed, and nobody will know what he reads from the book of magic, but when he opened his eyes, Magi looked at him with her eyes open, watching him with wonder.

He kissed her on her forehead and said, "I believed that you will wake up, my child. I'll go and call your mama."

In the morning, the castle came back to life. There was good news to celebrate, Magi woke up and was healthy as ever.

Gasper ate good portion of meat and was chewing the best bone that cook Teddy saved for him. The spell wasn't that powerful, so after sleeping for a few hours, Gasper woke up by himself with a hearty appetite.

"Because of your stupid broken leg, we even couldn't see where Apollonius went," Burak was muttering.

"I didn't break it on purpose, it just happened. If you didn't crash into me, maybe my leg would be in one piece."

"The secret book will remain a secret," Burak bit his lip peering into the darkness.

Suddenly, he saw a pair of small yellow-brown eyes gazing at him.

"Aah," he shuddered out loud, who the hell are you?" He addressed to the eyes peering at him.

"I'm a night creature," the creature squeaked in a revolting voice. Master Crowell calls me 'Hook.' He sent me here to take you home."

"I see only small eyes. How big is the rest of you? There are two of us and my partner has a broken leg."

"I'm not big, but I have large wings," the creature squeaked.

"Who are you anyway?" Burak said with squeamishly because it must be a disgusting creature, to have a voice like this.

"I'm from the bat family, my name is Hook," he repeated squeaking as his eyes moved closer.

"Climb on my wings and hold on very tight because the wind can blow you away and you will fall. There is no way to survive for creatures like you who doesn't have wings."

"Thank you for advice and warning, now I'm not only afraid of Gamut, I'm now afraid to fly."

"Nothing can be worse than to face Master Crowell when we arrive," Gamut added, grabbing onto Hook's wing.

"Ready?" the bat squeaked.

"Go," Burak commanded.

Hook soared in the air, and they flew up in the darkness. Then the crescent of the moon appeared in the sky. The night was very dark and it was very cold up in the air. As soon Hook flew out from underground, he sharply changed the altitude downward, and both riders rose in the air and almost lost their grip.

"Aaa, I can't hold on," Gamut shrieked because his legs were straight up in the air and his fingers started to lose grip. Hook climbed a little bit, and Gamut's body was once again on his wing.

All the way to the castle, they were bouncing up and down, swinging their whole bodies from side to side, any minute they could lose grip and fall.

Hook soared in the air, and they flew up in the darkness. Then the crescent of the moon appeared in the sky. The night was very dark and it was very cold up in the air.

This is a nightmare," Burak shouted and saw Gamut separate from the bat with a piece of Hook's wing membrane in his hands. Burak sees the hole in the wing and Hook was losing altitude. Gamut was falling, and Hook sped up, made a circle, and flew under Gamut. Burak slid from the wing and flew on the air still holding on the wing. Gamut dropped back on to Hooks wing and grabbed it with a death grip. Hook made a maneuver to bring Burak back onto the wing.

Finally, Hook started the descent. "Smack, smack," their bodies made slamming sounds. Both of them hit the roof of the castle. They rolled off the bat's wing onto the tiles of the roof, and Hook took off barely staying in the air because his wings were torn.

The roof had a big slop and Gamut was sliding down. Burak grabbed him to hold, but it was nothing for him to hold on and they both were rapidly sliding and in a split moment, both were falling. Gamut was hanging and barely holding onto Barak's legs when Burak grabbed the gutter at the edge of the roof. The gutter was too corroded to hold their weight, and they fell from the second story with the piece of gutter following them.

"Aaa, Aaa," both screaming so loud that whole city must have been woken up.

"Ouch! Ouch!" they fell onto their backs with a muffled sound, spreading their arms and legs. Gamut managed to hit Burak in his face with his broken leg. The corroded piece of gutter landed on his face, spreading corroded dust all over them.

"Damn you, Stupid," Burak shouted, whipping blood on his sleeve from his bleeding nose.

"Ooh, you broke it," he was shrieking.

He swung his hand and slapped Gamut in his jaw.

"That for the broken nose," he spits out the disgusting powder with a taste of corroding metal.

They were laying and groaning for some time.

"Get up," he pulled his useless partner up from the ground and Gamut stood on one leg. He tried to jump on one leg, but it was hard to do on grass.

"Climb over," Burak slouch over to give him his back to step on and then dragged Gamut to the Castile's doors, muttering all the way.

Inside, Crowell was waiting for them. His bulging eyes looked more cross-eyed than ever. His ferocious voice rooted them on the spot. He was holding his long twisted wand with a sharp point.

"You two useless chumps," Crowell was yelling and splattering. "Go away from my sight or I...," he banged his wand on his palm.

As if hit by a strong wave, both of them were swept away from the hall. They got to the room which they shared with the other two students and collapsed on their beds in exhaustion.

"Uh, what a nightmare," Burak, sighed falling a sleep.

"Tomorrow will be worse than this night because Crowell will deform you."

"Oh, it's painful," the boy from another bed said, "He did it to us last week, I still can't get over it."

"Oh, omnipotent devil, save us," Gamut was whispering before he fell asleep.

Crowell didn't have enough pupils to give them a rest or to disable them. So, Burak and Gamut were lucky to be spared being deformed for now.

He found the way to use them in their poor condition.

In the morning he called them to his spacious room and gave them assignment.

"Write on a piece of paper the names of all the people who live in Apollonius castle, including the gardeners and grooms at stables. Additionally, to the names, write the affirmation if they are already dead.

"Oh, don't look at me like that. How many times do I have to tell you the same over and over? Ohhh," he sighed, shaking his head, and then repeated his lesson from last week one more time.

"The spirit will think that the person already died, and he will prepare for the soul's arrival. Such will be the force of this believe among the spirits connected with receiving departed souls. Their concentration will attract the soul of the body of the person's name, and he will die, you got it?"

"Uh huh," the useless creatures nodded with their heads.

"Not one of the doomed men should know that his name has been placed before the spirit, or he will expire from the fear."

"Where do the papers with the names go?" Burak dared to ask.

"It's not any of your business. Just prepare the papers."

The assignment was secret even from the other students, so they were locked in a small room that must have been a closet before because the entrance was from the Crowell's room. There was room for only one table and two chairs.

Burak heard that he was talking to somebody in his room and he looked through a hole in the door and listened. The room was full of ghosts sitting at a long table, and he heard what Crowell was saying.

"Go tonight, place a paper in each coffin, and then leave unnoticed, got it?" He walked around the room and was talking to himself.

"After they are secured in the stinky coffins, the castle will be ours, and it will be easy to get the book," he clapped slightly with his hands, being satisfied with his plan.

Chasing the Ghosts

Atony took a nap, and at midnight, was ready for their night adventure.

Through a small opening in their door, they could see the ghosts are filtering through the wall at the front of the castle.

"What is that they are holding in their hands, everyone has it?"

"Looks like a folded paper."

"It looks like they have a plan and must be the nasty one. We better be prepared."

"Before I went to bed, I noticed a box under your bed. I never saw it before. What's inside it?" Atony asked.

Rocco had a wondering expression on his face.

"What box? I have no idea what you are talking about."

They went back to their room, pulled the box from under Rocco's bed and opened it.

"I don't know where this box came from; it must be some magic."

"If it's magic, it means that everything inside has magic power."

He opened it. "Hey, it's shoes. Let me try them on. He slipped one of his feet into a shoe, It fits perfectly and is very soft." Rocco stood on his right leg and jumped." Whoa," he went high in the air. "They are jumpy. Here, try another one on your left foot," he gave it to Atony. "Great," Atony jumped, "The shoes have wings, and they will be very helpful to chase the ghosts."

They pulled all contents out of the box. There were precious gems, blue feather, dice, and bag with silver drops, and crystals. "I like it," Rocco took the crystal and squeezed it in his fist.

"Look, there is a bee inside a jar. It must be dead," Atony examined the bee.

"Let me see," Rocco took the jar in another hand.

"I wish we had not one, but many bees; they could help us to chase the ghosts out."

"Rocco, look its magic, the bee is not dead. It's alive!" And look, it split and has become two bees.

"They both doubled, now it's four of them and are they doubling too."

"Wow, we have an army of them!" Atony got excited.

"Just great! My pockets are full. If we need more things, we will have to come back to get them. Let's go now, or we will be late, and the ghosts will do something bad. There are too many of them already in the castle."

"Can you see any ghost around?" Rocco asked in a whisper.

"Not here, but I see them gathering next to the wall."

"We already wasted too much time; follow me," and Rocco climbed over the rail of the staircase and slid down. Atony was behind him, and they landed softly on the floor with one shoe on.

Slightly bouncing on the special shoe, they got deeper into the hall and hid behind a column.

"What are they planning?" Atony wondered.

"Do you remember the night when they were storing the coffins in the music room? It looks like they are going to do something with it today."

"And the folded papers they brought with them tonight have some connection to it. We have to stop them from doing whatever they are going to do with it."

"You right. I'll throw the gem at that one to draw his attention, and you run to another column. We need to get closer to the music room," Rocco whispered.

"Wait when he gets closer."

Rocco threw a red gem and hit the shoulder of a ghost. The ghost made a gurgling sob. The gem must have burned a hole in him because even through his hand the hole was visible.so he covered the hole with his hand. The gem landed behind him on the floor, and another ghost picked it up. He made a frightening squeak, abruptly jerked his hand, threw the gem and hit another ghost.

"It must burn them through. They all had visible holes where the gem touched them."

"Ha, ha, it works."

The ghosts were running in the hall completely disoriented and were dropping the papers on the floor.

"Keep going," Rocco got excited.

They threw gems, one by one, and most of the ghosts had many holes in their bodies.

"I don't have any more gems."

"Here, throw the silver drops."

 But silver drops had a different effect.

"Look, that one is holding his stomach and looks like he is laughing."

"What possessed them, they all laughing."

"I don't know, but it's the time to let the bees loose.

"Yeah," Atony stretched his lips into a wide smile. "Free the bees," and he opened the jar."

"It looked like a Genie emerged out of Aladdin's lamp, a cloud of bees swarmed in the hall and were stinging the ghosts.

The ghosts were jumping in the air, slapping the bees with their hands, but their hands went through them. The bees flew away and stung them in the leg, or butt, or neck.

The ghosts panicked and were running like lunatics in circles, bumping into each other, falling to the floor full of pain or laughing hysterically. The bees continued stinging them more and more.

"They lost their papers, the bees are doing a good job because the ghosts forgot why they came here," Atony said with satisfaction.

Both boys were excited that they couldn't stand still behind the column and were jumping high in the air watching the chaos they created.

The ghosts noticed them and ran toward them.

"There is no way you can catch me," Rocco shouted. He put his hand in his pajamas pocket and pulled out the blue feather. That made a big impact on a skinny ghost who was very close to Rocco. The underfed ghost that Richy named 'Bone,' turned around and ran as fast as he could. Rocco followed him and tickled him under his buttocks. Bone was skipping like a grasshopper, making shrill noises. The other ghosts didn't waste any time.

Now they were chasing the boys who were hard to catch because they were bouncing like balls, flying high in the air, and were untouchable.

The boys ran into the music room, and ghosts followed them. They wanted to run back to the hall, but the ghosts blocked the doorway.

"We're trapped," Atony shouted.

The skinny ghost, Bone, growled and showed his mouth full of teeth. He almost reached Rocco with his bony hand, but Rocco jumped and hung in the air. Bone headed after him, trying to grab Rocco's leg. Atony went into the air and pushed Rocco to another side of the room to save him. The other ghosts were watching the chase for a while, and one by one got involved in the deadly game. It was hard to stay in the air, and boys bounced themselves between walls.

Trapped in this small room full of ghosts and coffins, the boys were absolutely exhausted. "Rocco, I can't hold any longer, there is no clean air left to breathe." Atony panted. Rocco himself was covering his nose and mouth from the stinky air.

"What to do? The crystal," came to Rocco's' mind. "What do I have it for?"

He squeezed the crystal hard in his wrist and said in despair. "Oh, I wish Aspar was here."

As soon as he thought of him, Aspar, squeezing between ghosts, showed up in the doorway.

The appearance of Aspar made a huge impact on hysterical ghosts.

They all were flailing backward, stepping on each other's feet, and stared with tense wonder at the black cat as he started to grow in size. Aspar gazed at them with his glowing jade-green eyes in the darkness of the room. Like being hypnotized, they looked at him with fear and started stepping back, falling over the coffins.

Aspar just sat there and didn't move. He must be taking his time.

"Why is he just sitting, we don't have time because the night will be over soon and who knows what will happen tomorrow?" Rocco though, "I have to do something."

Seeing the confusion between the ghosts, Rocco took his chance. He descended on the floor next to Aspar and pulled the blue feather out of his pocket.

He got closer to Aspar and elevated a little bit over the floor. Then he tickled Aspar's nose.

Aspar opened his mouth very wide.

"Achoo," he sneezed with such force that it was like a big explosion. It shook the air, and all ghosts together with the coffins flew to the wall and through it.

Momentarily, the air in the room became fresh.

"Oh," all three of them took a deep breath, closing their eyes with delight and relief.

"I can't believe how stuffy it was in here," Atony said, feeling dizzy from fresh air.

"They are gone for good," Aspar said, shrinking to his normal size.

"Let's go to the hall to see what papers they left behind," Rocco said and picked up one. He opened it and read the name, Apollonius. Then tried to follow the words that were in such bad handwriting that even Apollonius himself wouldn't be able to figure out what it said.

They collected all papers. "Tomorrow will be another day, and we will read them tomorrow."

"I'll go to take a nap," Aspar said yawning and rubbed his head around the Atlantis shoe on Rocco's right foot.

"What a night," Atony said hitting the pillow.

"It was quite entertaining, a?" Rocco said, falling asleep. Good night, Atony, tomorrow will be another day."

The end

Richy closed his notebook. He just finished on time because next day the competition started.

The Competition

Every year it was a big event and in the main auditorium where a thousand students took their seats. This month the fifth graders were competing between 5A, 5B, and 5C groups. Every student read his or her story from the stage in front of all the school. A hundred and twenty-one students were participating in the competition. By tradition, next month, the sixth graders will compete between their groups and then seven graders and so on.

All stories were short, and most of them were about house pets.

The stories of Barbes and his gang were about violence and fighting. When Barbes read his story, he enjoyed describing the bloody noses of his enemies, and it was gross.

Richy's composition was the last one because it was the longest. It took a while to read it, and the audience was captivated by the story.

There was no doubt that he won. When he finished the story, he received a trophy. The principal handed him a heavy bronze open page book that was attached to the base. The audience enthusiastically applauded, and Richy was the star of the day.

The story was so good that it was adopted by the theater group in school and was a play was made from it. It was such a big success that the students were invited to perform on a big stage in the city theater. "Searching for Magic" by Richy Knight, the headlines were screaming "a hit" on the front pages of all the newspapers.

Richy Knight became famous. His name was in newspapers saying, "So young and so talented." His name was mentioned in conversations throughout the city. He has announced as the best student of the year.

His father took the story to a publisher and Richy worked hard to polish his story, which was printed and sold in all stores all over the country, abroad, and of course in his father's bookstore.

Richy was very happy with his success, but it didn't make his head get too big. He was the same boy, only one year older, and now was eleven and half years old.

The Summer Vacation

Richy spent every summer vacation in the city which was filled with heavy smells and large crowds. To his surprise and delight, he was invited by the city to spend his vacation in a summer camp. Only the children of the rich and privileged could afford to spend summer in camps like this.

Of course, he will miss his closest friends Nicolas and Philip, but there is always a chance to make new friends.

Richy's small chest with his clothes and personal things was loaded onto the top of a carriage, and it was time to say goodbye to his family. He looked around in his room one last time to make sure he didn't forget anything important. Of all his treasures, he decided only to take his Crystal with him. Asap was rubbing his head on Richy's feet. "You are so smart," Richy said stroking Asap's back. "I wish I could take you with me, but I can't. I won't forget you, don't worry."

"I'm not worried," Aspar said. "I'll always be with you."

Richy took his seat with the adult passengers in a carriage driven by four horses and looked out the window. Soon, the city changed to a countryside. Richy was looking through the window as the trees were slowly moving back. The carriage was jolting on a dusty road. The picture became monotone. He pulled the Crystal out of his pocket and played with it, rolling it in his hands. His mind was wondering about many things.

He thought about the book of the astrologer and physician Doctor Michel de Nostradamus, he read in his father's bookstore, just before his departure.

This incredible individual was born at the beginning of the 16th century in France. Nostradamus was a man of equal, if not greater, fascination than his prophecies. "Physician, linguist, scholar, diplomat, writer, teacher, and profit, he contributed enough to earn a place in history.

This great genius predicted many wars and natural disasters and things that are interesting to Richy. Things like a giant snake made of metal that rapidly spread over the earth to deliver good and bad things and much more.

Richy's fantasy didn't have a limit. He was already moving with the snake to unknown lands.

He must have taken a little nap, or nap took him, but he found himself not sitting on the same seat and in a different carriage. He was alone in a cubicle the size of a small carriage and the window was different, thou the landscape didn't change much.

He didn't have time to figure out where he is and what is going on as the noise of sliding door took his attention.

In the doorway was standing a boy. His black eyes and curly black hair were standing out.

"Are those seats taken?" the boy asked.

"No, please, I'll be happy to have you here," Richy said with delight to have a company.

The boy walked in carrying a leather case.

Richy stood on his feet to help the boy with his case, but to his surprise, another identical boy walked into the compartment. Richy shook his head to be sure that his eyes were not experiencing double vision.

"My name is Rocco," the boy smiled and stretched his hand. "Don't be too surprised. This is my twin brother, Atony. Even our parents sometimes can't see the difference between us," he giggled.

"You s..s..s..said your names are Rocco and Atony?" Richy was stuttering in astonishment and dropped onto his seat in disbelieve.

"Yes, what's wrong?" Rocco asked, pushing his case under the seat.

"What a coincidence," Richy thought, "I named my heroes in my composition Rocco and Atony, and they were also twin brothers." They both had curly brown hair and brown eyes just like them only these twin's eyes and hair are a little bit darker than he imagined them.

He sat for a while thinking about it. Both boys finished storing their cases and were looking through the window. The landscape was changing very fast as the train increased the speed. "They are comfortable in this carriage," Richy thought, still confused with this strange development.

Finally, boys took their seat across from Richy.

"Are you from Paris?" Richy couldn't hold his silence any longer because this strange coincidence consumed his thoughts.

"No, we are from Sibul," Rocco said smiling.

"What?"

"What? Did you hear about the country Medea?" Both boys were surprised that their companion was asking strange questions.

"Aaa, Medea," Richy decided, not to look stupid anymore and pretended that he just didn't hear it well the first time. "Of course you are from the capital of Medea, Sibul."

"Uh huh, both boys nodded their heads.

More puzzled, Richy decided to take a risk and asked, "How is your sister Magi, is she alright?"

Now both brothers were very surprised. "Do you know Magi?"

"Of course, I know all your family, your father Apollonius is a very famous magician, and the whole world knows about him."

That didn't surprise them at all.

"Are the ghosts gone for good from your castle?" Richy's said to surprise the brothers again.

Their eyes got completely wide open, and they heaved their necks in astonishment. "How do you know about the ghosts?" they said at the same time.

"There is a mystery in everything, isn't there?" Richy asked instead of giving an answer.

There was a knock on the door and conductor, a heavy set woman in a railroad uniform, walked in.

"Your tickets, please."

A wave of fear splashed on Richy's body. "The ticket?" He didn't remember purchasing a ticket.

The Conductor punched a hole in the brother's tickets and said. "Aaa Richy Knight, your ticket is taking care of," and she walked out closing the sliding door behind her.

Richy's eyes made a wondering movement, and he smiled to the brothers and said, "You see there is no problem with my ticket." To his surprise, the boys didn't ask any questions.

The twins got used to having magic in their lives, and they accepted this new situation as normal phenomena.

Now they had time to recall what happened in the castle before they left and all three of them were hysterical about how the ghosts were run off with the help of Aspar.

Good time goes fast, soon the train slowed down and stopped.

The three of them were the only the passengers who walked out of the train on a short wooden platform.

"Hello, my name is Sam. I guess you are going to the Sunshine Camp," the young man, not older than nineteen, addressed the group.

"Yes, we are," they said together.

"Then let's go. It's in walking distance. The camp is behind those trees," he pointed at the trees right in front of them.

"Do you need help with your cases?" the young man asked kindly.

"No, we can handle it. It's only summer clothes inside; there's not much else. We know that a uniform will be provided for us," said Rocco. Richy assumed that this was not the first time the twins were here. the brothers are not here for the first time. How else would they know about the uniforms?

Behind the trees was a three-story, long building made of yellow stones. The building looked very simple, but oddly, the roof has many black cones placed on it for whatever reason.

"That is boy's dormitory," Sam explained, "but you need to register first," and he led them to the administrative building. Two wide columns supported the heart shaped lintel over the entrance. They passed a big room with stone walls and walked through a hall to an office where a woman with hair that looked like ropes was sitting at an old table. She got up and said with a sweet voice, "Welcome to Sunshine camp. You can address to me as Mrs. Medusa. I'm the director of the camp." She opened a thick old book with tattered pages and checked their names. "Sam will show you your room," the director said with an unnatural smile on her foxy face.

They followed Sam to the second floor of boy's dormitory through a long corridor. 'BURGAMS,' Richy read the sign on one door they passed, and then they reached the door with the name 'ASPARS' on it.

"Hmm," Richy said to himself. "What a day of coincidences, Aspar was the name of the cat in the castle, in my story."

They walked in, and there was a few beds in the room. "Six," Richy counted.

"These three are available," Sam pointed to the beds next to the door.

"Great, we will take them," Rocco said to Sam. Then he turned to Richy and said. "Have your choice."

The kind gesture made a big impression on Richy. Rocco will be my best friend, Atony comes with Rocco, anyway, they look and act as one person.

Richy chose the bed next to the door, which in his estimate was in the worst spot.

Sam was standing in the room to see that the new arrivals are comfortable.

"The closets are here for your cases, and you can choose a uniform that fit you. But if you prefer to wear your own clothes, that will be all right." He showed them the dressing room. "Here is the washroom and the rest of what you need."

"Where are the other campers?" Rocco asked.

"They are on a hiking trip and will be back for lunch. You are free till lunch to go around and to see the camp. After lunch, there will be other activities. See you later," and he walked out.

"There are the other buildings in the camp; they are for girls. They live only five in the room," Atony said. "Do you want to see?"

"Of course," Richy was now certain that brothers had been here before and they know the place very well.

They went outside and walked around the other five, one-story red stone houses with black cones on the roof.

"What are the cones for?" Richy asked.

"That is Mrs. Medusa fantasy. They added them three years ago to the flat roof."

"Last summer, there were only fifteen girls in the camp, the rest were boys," Atony kept on with the conversation, "This is a great place, you will like it. There's always something happening; you won't be bored, that is for sure."

On their way back to the building, they met a few boys and girls going to their rooms.

"Let's go to the cafeteria, I'm starving," Rocco said rubbing his empty belly.

The hall with very high ceilings, they call cafeteria, was huge dining place. The cafeteria was full of boys and girls, and they all were close to their age. They were making a lot of noise, standing in line with trays to get the food they desire from the buffet. The choices of food were incredible, salads, cold appetizers, hot steamy food under covers, different drinks, and much more.

"Yum, a lot of sweets," Richy noticed.

All three boys cleaned their plates that they brought to the table, sharing some fruits and pastries.

"Miss Maguey," one girl called out seeing a woman dressed in same sand color uniform as many campers. "Will it be a horseback riding lesson today?"

"Who is asking me?" Miss Maguey turned her head.

"Umm, it's you, Deana Camrusera. Yes, it starts at two o'clock," Miss Maguey answered to her, and then turning on her heels, walked out from of the cafeteria.

"Why are you staring at her?" Richy heard someone talking through his nose. He glanced at the boy, and his jaw dropped from bewilderment because the boy was a carbon-copy of Barbes. He looked up and saw mostly the nose. The protruding large nose was talking to him because the little mouth under the nose was so small, that it was almost invisible. When the boy passed Richy, brushing him with his elbow, Richy

was so small, that it was almost invisible. When the boy passed Richy, brushing him with his elbow, Richy noticed that his profile with nose and the upper jaw had a shape of a big triangle.

"Holy Mackerel," Rocco whispered so that only the two boys could hear him. "His nose got even bigger since I saw him last year."

"Who is the owner?" Richy leaned over the table, not to be heard.

"It's Burak, Burak Beset."

"W-what?" Richy expressed wonder on his face like there was something unusual about the boy's name.

Both boys widened their eyes.

"Oh, nothing, nothing, I just didn't know that he has a last name," Richy remarked clumsily.

The corners of Atony's mouth moved down, expressing surprise. "Everybody has a last name. Ours is 'Porpusales.'"

"Oh," Richy smiled. "Now I know your family name as well." Playfully, he said, "I'm...,"

"Don't be silly, Richy Knight, the famous writer; everybody knows your last name."

"No need to say anything more. I'm in a wonderland," Richy's mind assured him.

"Shall we take a horse ride this afternoon," Atony proposed.

"That would be great," Richy said. "I've never ridden a horse."

At two o'clock, the three friends were at the horse stables. Deana was already there and was talking to her horse in soft voice.

The horse guide, Petrus, was with the group of campers helping them to find the right size of boots.

Burak was one of them.

"Hey, Gamut, this will fit you, try it on" he shouted to a boy who had a face that only mother could love.

Richy was shocked again, learning about Gamut, but didn't express his wonder to any one this time. Actually, it became more interesting with every minute.

"I don't know how Gamut can see anything because his narrow eyes are hidden under a half sphere forehead on the top, which almost meet with a snub nose from the bottom. I never thought about any of my heroes how they look, but now I know," Richy thought. They are prototypes of Barbes and Godat at home.

"It's too small," his big lips moved, hiding his tiny chin.

Gamut couldn't find a larger size and used the ones he could manage to cram his feet into.

The group was dressed up in boots and everybody got a horse.

A strange thing happened at the last moment; Deana walked to Richy and asked him to exchange her white horse for his brown horse with three white dapples on her sides.

"I like the dapples," she said.

"I don't mind," said Richy and held his horse for Deana to mount.

Instructor Petrus explained that to begin with, they will climb the hill, and then they will descend the other side and walk around the hill to return to the camp. The trip will take good two hours.

Deana's horse was following the instructor's. She was ahead of the group and Richy Knight followed behind her. After him, Burak Beset, the Porpusales brothers, Gamut, and the other six campers.

Burak didn't like having to follow Richy instead Deana as he was planning. Richy didn't plan anything. He even didn't pay attention to who was behind or ahead, of him. He focused on learning to ride the horse.

Burak was pushing him when there was no place to go because the path up the hill was very narrow and it was a steep fall on the left side of the path.

"I have a feeling that something bad is going to happen," Richy thought. "It's good that my Crystal is always with me. I wish my horse could fly, just in case."

Richy could hear that the horse behind him was very upset. He looked back and saw Burak's horse standing on its back legs with the front legs up in the air and its mouth open with its tongue sticking out. And then Burak's horse kicked Richy's horse. All of a sudden, it didn't look like a horse to him anymore. It looked like Chimaera, a fire-breathing monster with the front legs of a lion, the body of a she-goat, and the tail of a snake.

Richy's white horse shuddered and soared into the air and spread her big white wings. "Wow," he said when he realized that he was not Richy anymore and that he became Bellerophon. He controlled his winged horse, Pegasus, with a golden bridle given to him by Athena. He swooped down toward the beast with an arrow and thrust a lump of lead between its jaws. The Chimaera's breath of fire melted the lead and choked her to death.

Pegasus returned to the ground and folded his wings.

Nobody saw Richy on the winged Pegasus except Rocco, Atony, and Deana. Everybody watched as Burak's horse fell onto her belly, and Burak flew over her head and tumbled under the cliff. He would have continued to fall if dry, dead bush wouldn't have stopped him.

"Ooooh," a groan echoed in the air.

Richy looked down and saw Petrus pull up Burak by his hand. Burak's legs were swinging in the air, and he was screaming like an injured beast.

"Hold tight, put your foot on that rock and try to pull yourself up," Petrus was shouting loud while pulling him up.

"What the matter with you?" Petrus scolded Burak when the ordeal was over. "You could have killed yourself and the others. Don't push your horse on the road like this; it's very dangerous."

The path became even more narrow and steeper.

"The best way to avoid accidents like this is to walk. Get off your horses," Petrus commanded.

Everybody was very scared of falling and was happy with the decision, except Gamut. His tight boots started to hurt his toes and heels. He was limping and groaning even louder than Burak who was bruised and scratched all over his body.

Burak and Gamut were not happy campers the remainder of the trip. More than that, they have to see a nurse to patch them up.

Lying on his bed with feet bandaged up on a pillow, Gamut was applying medicine on Burak's wounds.

"Did you see that Deana exchanged horses with Richy Knight?" Gamut twisted his smile, showing his two oversized front teeth.

"Oh, shut up, Moron. It hurts enough without your stupid remarks," Burak rumbled.

"Hey, cripple, are you going to get your mail, today is Monday?" their roommate Snick pushed his head in the crack of a door.

Once a week, the train stopped at the Sunshine platform, and Sam, as usual, brought the mail to the room next to the cafeteria.

"I rather relax and get it later, but Mr. Crowell never misses a week. He has to bother us, even on our holidays," Burak muttered.

"Yeah, he never leaves us alone," the big lips agreed.

"I'll do you a favor and bring your mail, but you'll be in debt to me," and Snick slammed the door.

"In debt, I need to teach him a lesson on being polite to me," Burak narrowed his eyes and squeezed his small mouth.

A few minutes later, Snick brought one letter for both, Burak and Gamut. It was of course from Mr. Crowell.

"There must be something important in the letter to seal it with devil's face," Snick said in an ingratiating tone.

"Go and mind your own business, Snick," Burak broke the black seal.

"STRICTLY CONFIDENTIAL," was stamped on the top of the letter.

Gamut made a move to join the reading.

"Stay there, it's confidential and secret," Burak stopped him. That only increased Gamut's interest, but he didn't dare to disobey.

Under the stamp, Burak read:

I got your letter from last week and couldn't understand your handwriting. Keep the letters separate from each other when you are writing.

I must repeat to you again that you are on a very important and secret mission. I'll be short with the explanation.

Once upon a time, the black magic kept the mortals under its power. The master of black magic, Golovorez, was sitting on the throne for many thousands of years. Mortals paid mass taxes and worked hard to stay alive. The empire of the black magicians conquered and occupied many lands and spread from ocean to ocean. That was a glorious time.

Then one figure proclaimed himself as a master of white magic and declared war on Golovorez. His name was Lunar.

Later you will learn about Lunar and how he became such a strong opponent, but for now, we need to act. It cost me a lot to get you in this camp, so you need to work for that.

The yellow stone building you are staying in is built over the ruins of an ancient fortress.

Under the ruins, there is an old lake where the sea monster, Mortelag has been trapped for many thousand years. The sea monster is the only one who survived till our days. Though it is a lake, it has salty ocean water, and that is why he survived for so many centuries.

He was overpowered by the white magic. The ancient magician Lunar, who by performing his tricks, clipped his wings, and without wings, the monster doesn't have the power to fight. We need to free him. Only he can bring to life our sleeping Lord, Golovorez and restore the Black Magic Empire. You will learn the rest of the story when you return home.

Your job is to bring food to the monster, so his wings would grow. He must be suffering from malnutrition by now. His favored foods are snakes, frogs, bats, mice, spiders, porcupines, and sometimes, mortals. Use the spells I taught you in class to put them to sleep.

Build a team to help you with the food, but don't give away the secret. For now, you can only trust Gamut.

Report back to me with the progress you make. Further instructions will follow after you succeed with the growing monster's wings.

Crowell

"Hey, Gamut, sit here on my bed," Burak commanded. "You need to read this letter."

Gamut, cursing the small boots giving him so much pain and limping on both legs, sat next to Burak.

They both read out loud every sentence of the important letter.

When they read the line, 'Report back to me with the progress you make,' the door made a squeak and slowly closed by itself. Burak crumpled the letter and threw it under his bed.

"Somebody heard us. Go and see who it was, hurry," Burak pushed Gamut from his bed.

Gamut limped to reach the door, but it was too late. Whoever was listening, now knows the secret.

"This is your fault," Burak, like always, needs to blame somebody for his negligence.

"We have no time to waste," Burak said, looking all business. "We need to collect the food and bring it to the starving creature."

Gamut, almost in tears, squeezed his bandaged feet into sandals. The blisters broke, and it hurt badly.

"Don't forget a sack for the snakes. I got one for the frogs."

"What about a team? It will be hard to collect a lot of snakes by ourselves."

"For now, we have to try without any help, and after all, who we can trust?"

They walked out of the building and made sure that nobody sees them head to the forest outside of the camp. They walked lazy, pretending they went for a pleasure walk.

On their way, they met Deana, who was walking from behind the trees with a bunch of yellow flowers.

". . . like flowers?" Burak stopped and asked through his nose. He always exaggerated his nasal tone when he wanted to impress somebody.

"Um, yes, yellow are my favorites," Deana said politely, giving a false smile.

"Yellow is my favorite too; they smell good. We are going to the forest to get a bunch for ourselves," said his nose.

Deana didn't trust what the nose said, and as soon they were behind the trees, she followed them. They were passing flowers and not picking any. What are they up to? Deana watched them from a distance.

There were no snakes or frogs around, but they were fortunate to find a hole in the ground.

"The mouse," Gamut whispered.

"Where?"

"He just went into the hole."

"Don't breathe, I will say the spell, "Abracatu- du-radimen-separrr, Abracatu-du radimen-separrr."

Burak muttered, barely moving his small lips, pointing his nose at the hole.

To their surprise, the mouse rose up from the hole and got out. Burak's spell, or his nose, helped, and the mouse collapsed on his side and stretched his legs. Burak collected the mouse by his tail, and overwhelmed by success, focused his nose on the hole and repeated the spell.

By doing it this way, they collected six mice.

"This will be enough food to start with," Burak said finishing with the hunting. "For now we will put the sack under your bed," he said to Gamut, "and at night, will look for the monster."

The rest of the day they spent time sitting on a bench and watching as two teams of twelve boys and girls were running after one ball.

"They have nothing else to do, this spoiled by their rich parents, loafers."

"Yeah and we always have to work, even on our vacation," Gamut was agreeing.

Snick was one of the players, and he was out of the game, so he sat next to his roommates.

"So, how many snakes did you catch today?"

"Snakes? It was mice we were after," Burak figured out that it was Snick, who was listening behind the door. He knows anyway, so it is a good opportunity to recruit him.

"Hey, Snick, you are the best person we know in the entire camp." Burak started in a warm and flattering voice. There is a reason you were placed to share a room with us. We are meant to be friends."

The words of recognition and acceptance made a positive impact on Snick. He moved closer to Burak and winking at him with one eye, and said enthusiastically, "I'll be your friend. You both remind me of my close friends from home, Barbes, and Godat. They even look like you. There's an incredible resemblance." Snick's eyebrows met on his forehead like he was trying to remember something but then gave it up.

"You must have heard what was in the letter from our Master Crowell. Tonight we will bring the mice to the Monster," Burak whispered because another player was out of the game and was approaching the bench.

"See you later," said Burak as he got up from the bench and Gamut followed him to the cafeteria to have a dinner. Soon after, the cafeteria was full of campers.

The three conspirators set together at one table.

"Look," Gamut kicked Burak under his elbow, spilling Barak's drink.

"Watch it," Burak growled. "What?"

"Deana set next to Richy Knight and the Porpusales brothers," for some reason I hate those two brothers. Their hair is as black as black cats have."

"Hmm," Burak nodded but didn't support the thought. His mind was preoccupied with the forthcoming night adventure.

After dinner, everybody went to the auditorium where dancing and singing was being performed on stage, which bored the trio to death. They retired to their room to wait for the night to fall.

As soon the light was off, they waited for their other three roommates to fall asleep.

"Aaa," a howling voice cut the air. The boy next to the window sprang from his bed and was on the window sill shouting "A mouse, a mouse is on my pillow."

Snick and the other boy with the squeamish squeal were on the top of their mattresses.

"They are all over the room," they screamed.

The mice quickly disappeared, but that didn't solve the problem. They were still in the room.

"Gamut, open the door," Burak shouted standing on his mattress with his bare feet.

"Open it yourself," Gamut shouted back.

You are a stupid idiot. You didn't tie the sack properly. Look at the sack; it has holes in it. Your spell didn't work. They woke up from your weak spell and nibbled through the sack; that's what had happened. You are an idiot yourself."

"I'll show you who's an idiot, and he tightened his wrist.

Gamut, jumping and skipping the steps, like he was running on hot coals, in a second, was at the door and ran far away down the corridor, leaving the door open.

All doors in the corridor opened at once, and a squeal filled the air because mice ran to all the rooms.

When the entire building woke up, somebody turned on the fire alarm and campers ran outside in a panic.

"It's a mice invasion," somebody was shouting. "There are thousands of them." The girls from the separate buildings joined the screamers.

"The situation is out of hand," one instructor was clapping with his hands for attention. The staff, including the foxy-face director Mrs. Medusa, Miss Maguey, Petrus, Sam, cooks, instructors, and the other adults was trying to calm down the campers.

"Sam," Mrs. Medusa was waving her hands, trying to shout above the squealing. "Turn off the alarm; it will wake up the demon underground."

Burak was near the foxy director and heard her mentioning the demon. "She knows about it," he accidently made the discovery.

The alarm stopped, and the noise started to calm down. Now they could hear as Mrs. Medusa was clapping her hands to get their attention.

"Okay campers," she said with a hoarse voice. "You scared the poor mice to death, and by now they are back in the forest to their holes. Go to your rooms; I assure you there is not a single mouse in the building."

All girls left the boys building, but Deana on her way out passed Richy and whispered, "I need to talk to you. Meet me tomorrow after breakfast at the tennis court."

"Right after breakfast, Richy was on the court. Deana walked directly to him and pretended to choose the right racket, said, "I saw them in the forest collecting mice."

"Who was collecting mice?" Richy asked with innocence in his voice.

"The big nose, he and his friend, Gamut, they were following me everywhere, so I decided to follow them to the forest and saw it with my own eyes. They brought the mice to the camp."

Richy didn't forget happened while horseback riding and he didn't like the 'big nose' since then. After all, he reminded him his neighbor and schoolmate Barbes and his buddy Godat.

"Looks as if they like to create troubles, we need to keep an eye on them."

"Don't worry; I'm following them, and they can't see me," she said with a smile.

"Be careful, they are not our kind of people," Richy said worryingly.

"I know that they can't use magic as we do."

Richy bit his lip. "You are...?" he raised his eyebrows.

"This one is good," Deana said when two girls came in and chose rackets.

"I just want to practice a little bit, I never played tennis before," Richy said, and they threw a few balls to each other, and were soon out of breath.

"They are together again, now playing tennis," Gamut said with a grin, exposing his two large front teeth.

"I will get to that later, we are facing a bigger problem, where and how to find the food to feed the monster."

"Yes, this is a big problem," like usual, a useless response from a useless friend. But good or bad, he was the only friend he had, so he shared his suspicions with him.

"I think that Mrs. Medusa knows about the monster underground in the lake."

"Really, how do you know?"

"She said the words that will wake the demon underground. It means that she knows."

"Go and ask her."

"Are you stupid," Burak said frowning.

But the problem to get the food for Mortelag didn't leave his mind. "After all, maybe it's only the way," he thought.

They started to follow Mrs. Medusa everywhere she went.

They saw her walking toward the kitchen. They didn't pay attention to the black and white cat which diligently washed his face in the corner of the corridor.

"Shhh, listen, she is talking to the cook," Burak and Gamut were hiding behind the door to the kitchen.

"Guys," Snick said trotting toward them.

"You will give us away, stupid." Burak gave a flick on Snick's forehead.

"Do you know who she is talking to?"

". . . to the cook, Stupid."

"To Mr. Medusa," Snick felt offended by not being appreciated for his discovery.

"It smells fishy," Burak whispered.

"It's not fish. He gave her a chunk of meat. Don't you see it?"

"Oh, shut up, Moran, of course I see the meat."

They held their breath when Mrs. Medusa passed them carrying the chunk of meat wrapped in a green bath towel.

They followed her till she closed the door of her office.

"Tonight she is going to feed the monster. We will be there," Burak said grinning.

"Uh, I almost knocked you down, Deana, what are you doing here?" Burak was surprised to meet Deana on his way again.

"Oh, the pipe in our bathroom burst and water is everywhere. I need to tell Mrs. Medusa. Have you seen her?"

"She just walked into her office," her answer soothed his suspicion that she might have heard them. Deana waited until the boys disappeared behind the door, and walked outside a little bit later.

"Deana, would you like to participate in a game to search for treasure? I'm gathering two groups," Miss Maguey addressed to her with a smile.

"I'd love to," she said, spotting Richy and the Porpusales brothers in one of the groups, and she walked to join them.

To take their mind off the forthcoming busy night and calm down the anxiety of his buddies, Burak joined the game. As expected, they were the part of another group.

"Let the game begin," Deana winked to Richy.

The game was very simple as Miss Maguey explained. Each group will hide their treasure, and the members of the other group will search for it, followed by a member of the opposite group to guide them with the words like freezing, cold, warmer, hot, very hot, until the treasure is discovered.

Each group was given a sack full of walnuts. One sack was small and the other bigger, but it didn't matter at the beginning. The group which finds the treasure first will get the bigger sack with more walnuts.

Mrs. Medusa as a neutral participant was asked to hide the treasures, and when she returned, she told each team where their treasure was hidden. And then the search began.

They played one hour, and there was no winner.

Snick was the guy who was guiding the seekers of the opposite group. He was lying to mislead the opponents. It was frustrating for the members of the big sack group, anywhere they went, Snick was saying "cold," but the lie was obvious to Deana.

"You are sneaky, Snick," she said to herself. "You are playing games with us, but let's see who will win."

Deana was the guide for the opposite group. She used her power of imagination in white magic. She switched the meat from Mrs. Medusa's office refrigerator with the big sack of walnuts which Mrs. Medusa herself hid.

Deana was following Burak, who used his nose to search the treasure, sniffing like a dog. "Warm," she said, "getting warmer, hot, very hot," her voice was rising.

Burak and his followers got excited. "It somewhere in here, Burak, go this way." His group supported him.

"It's burning," Deana was excited as well.

"Ah," Burak shrieked with a beastly scream and bounced back, knocking down the boy behind him.

"What is it?" Everybody gazed at the green towel. "What's inside? Where is the sack with walnuts?"

Burak brushed the seekers with his arms and ran as fast as his legs could carry him.

"What is it?" the boys and girls were asking in overly excited voices.

"Something wet; we need to tell Miss Maguey." Deana suggested.

Miss Maguey was already walking toward them.

"Miss Maguey, there's something wet inside this towel," the boys and girls were pushing each other to see what is inside. Miss Maguey prodded with her finger in a few places.

"Looks to me like it's some part of a dead body."

"Don't touch it. I'll look to see, Mrs. Medusa."

In a couple of minutes, Mrs. Medusa was storming toward them.

"Oh," she exclaimed in shock, covering her mouth and her eyes popped out of their sockets. "How did it get here?" she was looking lost.

"What is it, Mrs. Medusa? Miss Maguey asked timidly.

"Never mind," she said acting strangely. She picked up the 'thing' and holding it with both hands, walked very fast to her house.

The rest of the day, there was a lot of speculation about the mysterious 'thing' in the green towel and the strange behavior of Mrs. Medusa.

"This is unbelievably terrible," Mrs. Medusa was staggered. "I put the meat in the refrigerator myself. How in the world it get there?" She tried to think who knew about the meat. "Nobody," she answered herself, except my husband, Mr. Medusa. No, no, he couldn't play a game with me. Or maybe he did?

Confused and upset, she decided to wait till her husband finished his kitchen work to ask him.

She saw the disturbed campers outside, "Hmm," what will I say to them? They are waiting for an explanation."

She put a "Do Not Disturb" sign on the doorknob, locked herself in her office, and squeezed her head with her hands. "Think, think," she pushed her mind. But that wasn't the worse part. She needs to feed the monster, or his roaring will be heard many miles away. It happened once when she still was a child, and her father missed the feeding time. "Oh, better not think about it," she ordered to herself.

Finally, she decided the best way to handle the situation with the campers and staff was just act like nothing happened and it will cool down by itself.

In the evening, when Mr. Medusa came home from his job, he swore that he doesn't have time to play games, and seeing her wife so upset, suggested that he will go tonight to feed the monster.

Haunting in the Swamp

The next morning was so hot and muggy that the scheduled activities were replaced with a trip to the old lake to take a swim and the news was announced over the loudspeakers.

"Maybe we can find some snakes and frogs there, they like water," Gamut mentioned timidly.

"Finally your brain is working in the right direction," Burak made a flick on Gamut's forehead. He loved to do it to show his superiority.

"Get your sack," he commanded.

"The mice made holes in mine," said Gamut with a guilty feeling.

"Here," Burak took off the pillowcase from Gamut's pillow, "This will work. It has printed flowers on it for camouflage."

"Why don't you use your pillowcase, it has yellow flowers."

For that response, he got another flick on his forehead.

The campers lined up in single file, and Mrs. Medusa led the procession. The members of staff blended in with the campers.

The lake was so old; it was more like a swamp than a lake. There was a small sandy beach where all campers gathered.

While the campers went to the water, Burak, Gamut, and Snick, was catching frogs. To their delight, there was an abundance of them in the swamp.

"Hey, Gamut, catch the fat one," Burak pointed at a huge brown, covered with spots and blisters, toad.

Gamut jumped after the toad, but it was gone.

"Uh," you missed the best one," Burak said in disappointment. "Hold the pillowcase; I'll do it myself, Mr. sluggish," Burak muttered diving in the tall grass.

Overwhelmed by success, Burak continued hunting and caught about two dozen medium and large frogs.

"Did you see that? It was a snake."

"Where?"

"Don't move; it's next to your feet."

Burak turned over a stone and saw the snake's forked tongue moving at a speed of lightning next to his heel. He didn't have a choice and very quickly said the overused spell to put the snake to sleep before it had a chance to bite him.

He pointed his nose at the snake and quietly said the spell, "Abracatu- du- radimen separrr." The snake shuddered, a convulsion ran from its head to the end of its tail, and she didn't move. But as soon Gamut stretched his hand out to take it, in the blink of an eye, the snake's fang bit his finger.

"Ouch!" Gamut jerked his hand back and put his little finger in his mouth sucking the poison and spitting it out. "It bit me," he screamed.

"Be quiet, you have to say the spell which will work on her," Burak said with confidence.

Gamut feverishly ran in his mind through the spells he knew and said the one he thought would work on snakes.

The snake dropped dead in an instant.

"At last you are good for something," Burak patted Gamut on his shoulder.

"Because you remember only one spell and use it on dogs, mice, but it doesn't work on snakes," Gamut had a chance to pick on Burak.

"Oh, shut your mouth. You could be dying from poison and still want to argue." Burak has to have the last word.

"Snick, get the snake, I can't do the entire job by myself," Burak wiped the sweat from his face.

"Hold the sack, Gamut," he said lispingly. "Snick put the snake in the sack with the frogs.

"Uh, it drained all my strength. It will be enough food for one meal. We need a plan to get the bats," said Burak, walking to the lake.

They barely got wet, when Sam whistled to get out of the water and get ready to go back to the camp.

"No time to relax and swim a little bit. It's all Cromwell's fault," Burak was muttering to blame someone for everything.

There was only one cabin to change out of the wet bathing suits and the girls used it first. Burak and his gang didn't have enough time to change, and they were in a hurry to leave unnoticed with the sack full of frogs and one snake.

Burak led the group; Snick and Gamut walked behind him carrying his flowered pillowcase with the monster's dinner.

They made it to the camp before everyone and stuffed the sack under Gamut's bed.

At lunch, they saw Aspar sitting at one table and talking in a whisper. Deana was giggling and was very animated.

Are they making a plot against us, or they know what we are doing? Burak was guessing while stuffing food in his small mouth. I need to send Snick to investigate.

"From now on," Burak said to Snick, "you will spy on Aspar. I believe they know something about us, find out what they know," Burak gave the assignment to the new member of his gang.

Returning to their room before the other roommates, Burak looked under Gamut's bed to be sure that the monster's meal is there.

"Oh," he clapped his hands and pulled out an empty pillowcase.

"Where are the frogs and snake?" he shouted in disbelieve.

Gamut slouched expecting a punishment, and it didn't hesitate to come.

"For the second time, you stupid dummy lost it," Burak flicked Gamut's scalp with his finger, and it made a loud 'thump' sound.

"I must have used the wrong spell," Gamut said feeling guilty.

An unpleasant thought struck Snick.

"The snake must have eaten the frogs," he said adding fuel to the fire.

"Ooooh," Burak threw his arms in the air and growled like a ferocious beast. What will I do with you, two Morons?" Burak was cursing in a rage.

"You, Gamut" he pointed at huddled up Gamut, "Will write to Master Crowell and explain everything in your words what you have done? I'm sick." He collapsed onto his bed, crossed his arms over his chest, and closed his eyes.

"Oh!" Snick shouted in the doorway to the bathroom and froze on the spot. Burak jolted and sat on his bed gazing at Snick.

"What, again?" Burak shouted in anger.

"The snake, the snake," he mumbled. "It's in the bathroom."

"Go and get it."

"You go," Snick said in a snit.

Burak went to the bathroom and saw the moving tail sticking out of the toilet bowl. The snake's head was already deep inside, and it was squeezing its fat belly, stuffed with frogs, into the pipe.

"Get her by the tale," Burak pushed Gamut on his back. "We can't let her get to the pipe."

"Oh, no," Gamut almost vomited seeing the picture of a fat snake in the toilet. He ran out of the bathroom and out of the room.

Snick was standing in the doorway to quickly escape in case Burak forces him to pull the snake out.

They both were a witness as the snake made it.

It was gone.

Burak grabbed his head with both hands, and for the second time, collapsed on his bed.

Snick was glad that the snake was gone and he won't be forced to deal with the disgusting creature. "I better go to spy on ASPARS," he muttered to himself.

For the rest of the day, there was nothing interesting to declare to Burak, and Snick was ready to leave his hiding place where he could see Aspar playing basketball.

Something unusual took his attention. The players were sending the ball to each other or a bucket, and never touched the ball. The ball was flying by itself and sometimes, stopped and floated in the air for a few moments, and then it continued moving as it was before.

It can't be real. He rubbed his eyes with his fists. "It must be the snake clouding my thoughts," he decided and walked away. In the distance, he spotted Gamut walking back and forth, shaking his hands in front of him.

"What's wrong, buddy?"

Gamut opened his hand, and Snick saw the dark purple swollen little finger. It wasn't little anymore; in fact, it was bigger and fatter than his thumb.

"Uh, uh," Snick whistled, "you need to go to see the doctor. I'll walk you." He kindly suggested.

The doctor gave Gamut a shot and said, "Maybe it's too late to save the finger and it possible that the finger needs to be amputated, or you might die in the case of gangrene setting in. Why didn't you come right away?"

"I was looking for the snake," Gamut said out of turn.

Snick noticed that Gamut's reason was going to lead to more questions and pulled him by a sleeve to leave the doctor's office.

Snick was so kind to him, and he even said, "If they cut off your finger, then Burak has to write the letter to the master Crowell by himself. You see, you have to look at this with a positive attitude."

"What are they shouting?" Snick wrinkled his forehead.

Five girls were running and squalling like they were stung. They were swept away in an instant from their view.

"Hurry, let's see what is going on," he pulled Gamut. "They went to the administrative building, and they heard girl's screaming."

"Mrs. Medusa, you have to come with us." The girls stormed into Mrs. Medusa's office. All five girls were talking at once, barely able to catch their breath.

"There's a monster in our toilet."

"The head is sticking out."

"A monster?" Mrs. Medusa's eyes popped out of their sockets.

"And it's pushing itself out."

"Eeee," all five girls were jumping in one spot and squealing, shaking with their arms and hands in disgust.

Mrs. Medusa began to rush about the room, clapping on her chest with her hand. Her face turned green and was not looking foxy at all.

"The monster, he must be hungry, or the meat wasn't fresh enough," she gasped.

The girls stopped at once and froze in place with open mouths and blinking their eyes.

What is she saying? They looked at each other.

"Mrs. Medusa," one girl said her name.

"Oh, yes, right away, at once, let's go," she pushed them out of her office.

"Has anybody else seen it?" She asked carefully, feeling that she already said too much.

"No, only us."

"That's good, that's good," she repeated. "Nobody else," she rumbled as she jogged behind the girls.

As they passed Snick and Gamut, the boys followed them to the girl's house. They couldn't go inside because no one was allowed to walk in there without an invitation, so they stood in the corner next to the window which was slightly open.

"At least we will find out what is going on," Snick said carefully following them.

Mrs. Medusa, ahead of girls, ran into the bathroom and turned her head to look at them.

"Where is it?"

"In there," the girls pointed to the bowl.

Mrs. Medusa lost her consciousness and collapsed on the tiled floor.

"Ah, Mrs. Medusa," the girls shouted.

"She is more scared than us. Let's pull her out of the bathroom."

Two girls took her under the arms pits and pulled her out to the bedroom. Standing on their knees, they sprinkled her face with water from a pitcher and waved air in front of her face.

She opened her eyes and giggled, "He, he. He, he, he," and started to laugh. She laughed rolling on the floor holding her stomach, rubbing her eyes with her fists so hard that they became red. The laugh was so contagious that girls started to laugh as well.

Then she took a deep breath to stop the laughter, sat up, stretching her feet and said, "If you call that a monster, then you haven't seen a real monster in your life...." She choked on her last word. She scratched her head, "What's possessing me to talk like this? I have to think before I say something.

"This is only a snake," and she got up on her feet and flewshed the toilet a few times. The snake disappeared, and she headed out. "All you needed to do was flewsh the toilet. We are surrounded by forest with all kinds of living creatures in it." Her foxy expression returned to her face, and she went back to her house.

The boys heard her last words about the snake in the toilet, and they heard that she flewshed it down the drain.

"Good news, at last, something to make Burak happy," Snick said enthusiastically as they were leaving the girl's house with caution not to be seen.

The girls, like a flock of twittering birds, flew out of their place and spread in different directions.

Girls will always be girls. They like to talk, and right away the five of them shared the news with the other girls.

Deana didn't waste her time to bring the news to the ASPARS about the snake, Mrs. Medusa's unconsciousness, and that the snake now is swimming somewhere in sewer pipes.

She found them on a bench under the tree. It was a safe place to talk secretly. Aspar was quietly sitting under the bench.

"So, Mrs. Medusa and her husband, the cook, are feeding some monster, which is living somewhere underground."

"We need to know what is going on there and where the monster lives."

"Right," Rocco said, "and we can use the snake to help us."

"But how?"

"I have some idea," Richy said, "Let's make the snake talk. If it can talk, it can also hear."

"Listen, hear, and talk," Atony said supporting his friend's idea. "But it will take time to teach it to talk. It might be better to make Aspar talk instead.

"Give us a minute," the brothers said to Richy and Deana. They moved to the end of the bench and just sat there quietly for a couple of minutes, and then moved back.

"It should work. Do you know what the snake is afraid of the most?"

"Porcupines," Atony said.

"And cats, big and smart cats, like Aspar," Richy added.

"Aspar," Deana repeated. She couldn't put together the sign in their room 'ASPARS' and the name of a cat they just mentioned, and she looked at Richy with a question in her eyes.

"Oh," Richy noticed her confusion. "He is an ancient cat from Egypt, and he was a part of Nefertiti's family and later served Tutankhamen," He briefly explained to Deana. "His original name is Asap. He is a miracle of a white magic. You will see."

Deana gave a smile to the boys of appreciating their friendship and trust.

From nowhere, a black cat with thick fur and jade-green eyes jumped onto the bench and rubbed his head on the boys and then did the same to Deana.

"Are you Aspar?" Deana asked him patting his shiny coat.

"Yes I am, hello, Deana," Aspar said with shyness in his voice and jumped onto the ground.

Deana followed him with her eyes as he walked to Snick and Gamut who were passing nearby and they saw that Aspar followed them.

"The snake wasn't lost; it was in the toilet," Gamut agreed with the good news.

"Let's go and see Burak now," Snick said as they walked some distance behind Mrs. Medusa.

They couldn't help but hear on the way back to her office; Mrs. Medusa was blessing all demons in the world and that it wasn't the monster who escaped from under the ground.

"He is safe, and I need to ask Mr. Medusa for an additional chunk of meat to treat our Lord better."

Hearing her muttering, they changed their plan to see Burak and followed Mrs. Medusa to her house. Her apartment was at the back of the house, and they stopped under a small half-open window.

When Mrs. Medusa is under stress, she always flosses her teeth because it gives her relieve and comfort. She just opened the door to her bathroom, and it was there. The snakes head was sticking out of bowl moving in motions to get free.

"Oh, my Lord, you are here?" she exclaimed in astonishment. She moved to flewsh the snake down as she taught the girls.

"Ssssss, you won't do it to me again, Mrs. Ssssss, Medusa," the snake was making threatening hissing noises with a whistling voice while shaking its head.

She flewshed it anyway, but the snake didn't go down. It got completely out and was hanging vertically in midair, waving with its body like it was held by some invisible grip next to her head. It was a strange looking snake because in the middle of her body was a bubble like some balloon was stuffed inside.

"Snakes are supposed to be a friendly creature to us, but this one is very unusual," Mrs. Medusa mumbled to herself.

Mrs. Medusa took a few steps backward until her back touched the wall.

"Uh, vanish from my eyes!" she screamed and demanded to the snake waving with her hands. Her face expressed the fear of getting bitten by a bewitched creature.

But the snake was moving in the same direction and stopped right next to her face.

"Who are you?" Mrs. Medusa shouted in agitation.

"Ssssss, free me. Ssssss," the snake was talking in a choking voice with her mouth closed.

"Free you? Are you out of your mind? I'm not holding you. Go away." Mrs. Medusa was waving her hands. "Leave me alone," she shouted loudly.

The door in bathroom opened with a jerk and Mr. Medusa stormed in.

"What is going on, who is attacking you?"

The snake moved to Mr. Medusa and froze next to his face. "Ssssss," it made in a threatening husky noise.

"Run," he shouted to his wife. 'Bring our cat, hurry."

Mrs. Medusa broke into a run and tripped on a rug. She got up and run outside to find the cat.

She didn't see her gray striped lazy pet, but she saw an unfamiliar black and white cat, which was walking toward her from her apartment. Without any questions, she thanked her Lord for sending her a cat, the moment she needed it, and grabbed the black and white cat by his belly. In an instant, she was there to rescue her husband from the terrifying snake.

When she rushed into the bathroom with the cat under her arm, the snake was lying motionless on the tiled floor, and Mr. Medusa said in calm voice, "It's all over, dear, and there's nothing to worry about."

"Did you kill her?"

"No, she just dropped dead by herself."

"What a weird thing. I hope nobody heard us. We need to be careful that nobody discovers the dragon. A lot of strange things are happening lately."

"You're right, dear," Mr. Medusa looked at the pale face of his wife. "You are under so much stress these days. Just rest tonight, and I'll go feed him by myself again."

Mrs. Medusa dropped the cat on a floor, and she headed to the door.

Aspar found his friends still sitting on the same bench.

"They didn't see me when I held the snake by its neck in front of their faces, but I scared them to death, Purr." Aspar purred with delight closing his eyes. "They believe that the snake is dead. I didn't destroy her in case you need her in future, Purr. But at last moment, I heard what Mrs. Medusa said to her husband. "When you bring the meat to the monster, take the dead snake with you as well. It will be a special treat for our Lord."

"So, what else did you find out?"

"Mr. Medusa is going by himself to feed the monster tonight and the snake will be its desert. That is all. Oh, I forgot, he asked Mrs. Medusa to set an alarm for a quarter to midnight."

Rocco patted Aspar, and he purred his heart out.

"You did a great job, Aspar," Richy said. "Now it's our time to act. And we need to do it tonight."

"It's very risky to all go together. The four of us can make noise and spoil everything." Rocco said.

"It would be nice to be invisible, Atony sighed. Our father taught us to do it, but it takes a whole week to concentrate on this to achieve it."

"I can help," Deana said.

"My uncle, Lunar, taught me a very simple trick to be invisible."

Richy lifted up from his seat and dropped back in astonishment, "Who did you say is your uncle? Lunar is your uncle?"

"Yes," Deana moved her shoulders up and down. "Do you know him?"

"Do I know him?" he repeated trying to put piece it together in his head. "Yes," he said. "He is my teacher." Deana raised her brows, "Your teacher?"

"Oh, no, not in school."

The Porpusales brothers were listening with interest.

"I saw him one day when Notre Dame was on fire, and he made magical rain to put the fire out. Then he saved me in the desert. I met him later underground when Margo was lost, and he gave me a crystal that has a magical power. It helped me a lot, and I always have my crystal with me."

"Let me see," Deana took the crystal in her hand, and it turned blue.

"Wow, how did you do that?" Richy asked.

"It's magic," she laughed. "You just have to think it's blue and it will turn blue."

Richy took crystal in his hand, and it turned red. Both brothers tried and every time the crystal changed color.

"I don't want to demonstrate it here, but trust me, if you hold the crystal and think that you are invisible, you will become invisible.

"Will we see each other?"

"Uh huh," Deana nodded her head.

"Is that simple?"

"Uh huh," Deana stretched her lips into a smile. "Only you have to hold the crystal in your hand."

"But, it will be a problem for all of us to go and to be invisible with only one crystal."

"I have my crystal bits on a necklace. I wear it sometimes to appear and disappear or for some other reasons. I'll take it apart and give you crystals so we all can go."

Roaring Mortulag

Gamut and Snick found Burak sitting at the table in their room with his nose almost touching the paper. He was diligently writing every letter with the help of sticking out tongue.

"Writing a letter to Master Crowell?" Gamut asked.

"The summer will be over if I wait for you to do it," Burak barked glancing at him and pointed his nose back to the paper.

"I can't do it anyway."

Burak noticed Gamut's bandaged hand.

"What happened to you?"

"You know, that stupid snake in the forest bit me."

"The Doctor wanted to amputate his finger," Snick inserted.

These words gave Gamut goosebumps. He looked at Burak.

"He doesn't have a heart," Gamut thought because Burak didn't say anything and went back to his writing.

They waited for Burak to finish his letter.

Burak didn't finish writing because all letters were mixed together, and when he tried to reed, it was just not readable. He stopped, nodded his head, and said, "Go on."

Snick and Gamut were interrupting each other and told him all that had happened.

Burak gave himself time to absorb the news, to evaluate the situation, and then made a decision, "Tonight, be ready for a big night. We are going to follow Mr. Medusa underground."

"To see the monster?" Gamut said bustling.

Burak closed his eyes and shook his head, showing that Gamut is not using his brain to think.

"Will you show up in front of the monster without food?"

"But we don't have food, mice, frogs, snakes, we've got nothing."

"So, who lives underground in darkness?"

"The bats!" Snick exclaimed. He was happy to be smarter than Gamut at least once.

"Bats, that's right. We are going to find bats underground and Mr. Medusa himself is going to lead us there."

The waiting time is always stretches forever. "Are they going to sleep tonight or not," he was thinking, lying in his bed fully dressed under his blanket.

When the other three of their roommates were sleeping, they stripped their pillows and tucked the pillowcases in their pockets to put bats in and left the dormitory unnoticed. They quickly passed the girl's houses and hid behind bushes next to the arch shaped entrance of the tower building.

About five minutes later, they saw Mr. Medusa stepped out of his house. He stopped for a moment and looked around and then he continued walking toward the entrance of tower building. He was walking slowly, slouched under a heavy burden on his back. They stopped breathing when he looked at the bush where they were hiding. Then they watched him slowly open the door. When he was in, they carefully slipped behind him, keeping some distance.

In the dim light of entrance, they couldn't see the black and white cat who was watching them. As soon they were gone, Aspar stepping softly on the stone floor, ran to his friends to say that it's time to go.

"It is risky business to face the unknown beast," Richy thought, and he checked in his pocket to be sure, that his crystal in there.

"Hold your crystals and imagine that you are invisible," Richy whispered, "Let's go." Aspar had his own power to be whatever he wanted to be, and he became invisible as well.

They stood behind Burak, Gamut and Snick who were hiding behind the doorway and watched as Mr. Medusa touched a stone on the wall. The camouflaged stone door moved inward and then slid to the side. Mr. Medusa walked in and the door slid back. The trio from BURGANS room waited thirty seconds and opened the door same way. From where the ASPARS were standing, they could see how BURGANS opened the door, and thirty seconds later, all four of them, and Aspar, were behind the door.

It was a labyrinth of corridors where the trio disappeared. Richy and his friends sped up not to lose Mr. Medusa's light from their sight. They walked through narrow corridors and passed a few chambers. There was barely enough light to find the way. They saw his black silhouette walking toward some straight edge on the horizon.

Though they were invisible, their bodies were solid and they must have made some noise because Mr. Medusa stopped, looked around, waited a little bit listening, but it was quiet and he continued walking. Mr. Medusa had a tiny lamp in his hand and that was only the guide for the friends.

Soon, the light disappeared, and if not Aspar's warning, all four of them would have fallen on the staircase. They moved slowly when they saw the light again. There was no end of the stairs. Finally, they stepped onto the sand.

Because Aspar could see in the dark, he was leading the group. He turned his head so they could see his eyes glowing in the dark and then stopped. They heard some noise in the distance. They couldn't talk to each other, but they all recognized the sound of water. They knew that they were at the lake.

The moving light stopped when Mr. Medusa put the lamp on the ground. He whistled a few times, not loud, and he waited. Slowly walking, they got closer to the water.

Suddenly a big splash of water reached their feet as a wave crashed on them from above. Richy barely stayed on his feet. He looked at his friends and they managed not to fall. He noticed at the top of stairs were the two luminescent dots of Aspar's eyes staring at them. Aspar didn't like water. And after all, he didn't know how the monster would react to the presence of a cat.

Then the giant head of a beast rose from the water, making huge wave. The wide open mouth of his protruding jaw had a large numbers of sharp teeth with two big fangs. The black tongue like a snake was sticking out and he breathed fire from his throat.

The beast roared like thunder, shaking his head and continuously growled. A cloud of forceful steam was shooting from his nostrils. His round bloody eyes threw lightning and they saw the head not of a serpent, not a giant bird, but a disgusting beast unknown to the world. His neck and chest were covered with fur or feathers, it was hard to say in darkness and the color was black and dirty green.

He was splashing water with incredible force and a giant wing rose over his head, but it was visibly clipped.

The berserk beast was splashing, creating big waves, which reached the group. But that was not all they saw. As soon as the fire from the monster's mouth gave light, they could see the giant serpent's tail and huge body rising and disappearing into the boiling water. The air smelled nasty. It was coming like a wave with every breath of this beastly monster.

Scared to death, they stood with their hands under their chin, shaking from the cold water and fear.

"What's wrong with you today?" Mr. Medusa shouted at the Monster. "It's only me with food. Calm down Mortelag; nobody is here."

The revolting monster continued roaring and breathing fire.

"He must be feeling our presence," Richy whispered.

Then they saw as Mr. Medusa pulled out the sack the food he brought with him and placed it on a big flat stone, which could serve as a dining table, or altar for sacrificing.

The thrill went through Richy's body, when he saw as the beast snatched a piece of meat with his sharp teeth, then with the help of his tongue, he send it down his throat. He tore another chunk of meat to bits with his sharp teeth and the rest was gone in an instant.

"The desert," Richy thought, and it came.

Mr. Medusa pulled the snake out of the sack and put it on the stone. The snake was wriggling but didn't live long. The black tongue licked it up in a blink of an eye.

Mr. Medusa stood for a while and watched the beast swing its head, spraying millions of cold water drops in all directions before diving into the dark abyss. Mr. Medusa turned around and walked away. He didn't know that he was accompanied by four invisible people.

If the four of them weren't wet from head to toe, they wouldn't believe what they witnessed. The devilish beast Mortelag exists, and he is right there under their feet. They returned to the outside the same way they came in.

"Thank you, Deana, for the crystals," Rocco and Atony wanted to return them to her.

"Keep them, I have plenty," and she disappeared behind the door in her house.

"Where are you going, Aspar?" Rocco asked when they reached their room.

"Oh, you know cats don't sleep at night; it's hunting time. I'll just hang around. Good night everybody," Aspar walked away swinging his tail in the air.

He walked into the corridor and noticed a crack in the doorway where Burak and his buddies were living. Their three beds were empty. He walked in and made a sweep around the room. There was a ball of crumpled paper under one empty bed, and Aspar couldn't resist kicking it with his paw. The ball made a rustling sound, and as he kicked it, he got in a playful mood running and kicking it till it was out of the room. That was his trophy, and he rolled it in ASPARS room under Richy's bed. Then he found a nice spot next to Rocco's feet and fell asleep till morning.

Camrusera

"They are coming," Atony whispered, sipping a cup of apple juice at the breakfast table.

"They look tattered," Deana said.

"They must have gotten lost in the labyrinth. They didn't make it to bed last night," Rocco added.

"How do I know?"

"Aspar told me this morning."

"It would be interesting to find out how much they know about the monster," Richy said, whipping his mouth with a napkin to tone down his voice because Burak was passing him carrying a tray with food.

"I need to go back to the room," Richy said, "to get the letter I wrote home, or I will miss Sam. He is collecting the mail today to take to the train."

The wind from the open window blew the envelope onto the floor, and Richy bent to pick it up. He saw the crumpled ball of paper under his bed and smoothed it to open.

The stamp "STRICTLY CONFIDENTIAL" screamed at him.

He read the letter very fast and put it in his pocket.

On his way, he picked up a few magazines from the table in the lobby and found his friends walking outside the cafeteria.

"I got something we need to read," he said. "Let's go to our favorite bench where nobody will disturb us."

Nobody noticed as he slid Crowell's letter between pages in Deana's magazine.

"After you read it pass it to boys," he whispered.

After they all had read the letter, there was a silence for some time. The electricity in their brains traveled through all cells at ones, gathering all impressions, memories, and information stored in their minds.

"Our father, the great magician Apollonius, told us many stories about the Golovorez's black magic Empire," Rocco was saying slowly, as he was trying to recall the memory.

"He also told us folklore about Lunar," Atony continued.

"Deana," Richy looked at her. "I don't know much about your uncle Lunar, but I'm fascinated by him. How did he become so powerful?"

It was as if Deana was waiting for Richy to ask her, she looked at him, and then turned her head straight, "Throughout your many lives Richy, you will meet with my uncle many times."

"Throughout many lives," Richy repeated. His eyes wide opened, and he peered at Deana.

Suddenly, her solid material face started to move and change. Gradually she transformed into somebody else right in front of his eyes. She reminded him of Serena. Richy blinked a few times to be sure that he what he was seeing was real. Aspar was also was fascinated by this incredible vision.

The 'image' was sparkling and glowing.

Her voice reached his ears from a far away distance and was echoing in an endless space.

She was standing on a rock peering into space, dressed in a long lavender dress with sparkles and was surrounded by an aura.

"She is Goddess Camrusera (the Goddess of magic), pumped into Richy's head.

Tingles went through his body. His jaw dropped; so magnificent and captivating she was. The precious stones on her dress blinded his eyes, and her hair looked like fire. She was holding a blue feather in her hand, and her eyes were staring into space.

The images from his memory passed in his eyes as he was seeing them again.

"So, in the cave in India, the gold statue in the temple in Mesopotamia, Serena from the Island, and Deana are the same Goddess of magic," Richy was stunned by discovery.

Her echoing voice returned him to the scene. She was talking into space.

"Through your experiences in life, you will find out about the invisible sphere, known as Daath...ath...ath...ath. The sphere is one of the greatest mysteries of the magical book. Its name is Knowledge...edge...edge...edge."

"So, the magical book I'm looking for is about knowledge?" Richy asked.

"Yes, the desire to know and have experiences makes people want to live. It keeps them young. As soon as the desire to know all is lost, a person dies inside. It is knowledge, and the first triad of spheres is known as Supernals defined as the state of super consciousness."

"Supernals," Richy was repeating without noticing it like he was hypnotized.

"To reach Supernals, one has to cross the broken line separating them from the other Sephiroth, the line or veil known as Abyss."

"Abyss," all three boys repeated, touched by magic.

"My uncle Lunar crossed that line, and he is in the womb of the universe, in other words, he became immortal."

"Immortal," all three boys repeated.

"Yes, he is immortal, and only immortals have unlimited power."

"Monster Mortelag lives forever, and if they feed him, he will never die," said Atony.

"They try to keep Monster Mortelag alive feeding him so he can grow his wing and restore power to their dark lord Golovorez," Rocco said supporting his brother's thinking.

"That is the hitch, and that's why he never will reach superpower."

Three pairs of eyes didn't blink, being captivated by the goddess's words waiting to find out, why.

"Because," the goddess said, "In order to cross that broken line, one has to give up all his material comforts and pleasures including food."

"So, the best way to make them fail is to help them to feed Mortelag."

Suddenly Richy sees Deana on the bench next to him and she said. "I don't know about you guys, but I'm on my summer vacation to rest and not to work."

"Wow," all three boys exclaimed at ones.

"How did you do it?" the Porpusales brothers asked.

"Did what?" Deana asked.

"Ah, never mind, Deana," Rocco said rising from the bench. "It's getting hot. Let's have some refreshment."

The Fun Game

In cafeteria on a cork board was a push-pinned paper announcing a game of Speedball, similar to volleyball, this afternoon.

"We can have fun," Deana said and winked to boys, walking outside with them, sipping a cold drink.

"Look," Atony pointed with his finger, "they are sitting on our bench."

"What's Aspar doing there?"

"He is listening of course," Rocco said, grinning.

Aspar spotted his friends and ran to share what he heard.

"Burak is going to use spells on the ball, and all of you during the game, so be prepared," Aspar blurted out and walked away.

"Thanks, Aspar."

"Don't mention it," he gave him a glance and waved his tail in the air.

The tall, skinny sports instructor, Dovry, was organizing the teams.

"Avon," he called his favorite athlete, the boy with the blond hair, "Where is Avon? Would you find him for me?" He asked Stanislaw, who was standing next to him.

Stanislaw returned without Avon, "Honesty, I looked everywhere, but couldn't find him. I even asked his for help to find him. His roommate said that he hasn't seen him since yesterday."

Stanislaw, you replace him for now, and then we will deal with Avon."

Like it should be expected Richy, Deana, and both brothers were in one team. They took name "ASPARS"

Burak, Gamut, and Snick were forming another group and they called themselves "BURGAMS."

The campers took their seats to watch and support the teams they chose. Mrs. and Mr. Medusa were watching with them.

All the girls became cheerleaders, and they were divided by Miss Maguey to cheer for their teams. Both teams had one girl playing, and the rest were boys.

Dowry blew a whistle to start the game.

The ball was in the air flying back and forth over the net.

The campers were swaying on their seats following the ball. The cheerleaders were jumping up and down waiting for the score.

The ball was flying right into his hand, and Burak jumped to smack it and send it down.

The ball hit the ground behind the net and rolled over the line before the players on the other side could touch it.

The cheerleaders in green skirts performed a short dance. Sam announced the score. Burak, with his nose up, walked around to give a "high-five" to his buddies. "That's the way to go," Snick said, smacking Burak's hand.

"Watch the ball!" Gamut yelled.

Hover Pucker, the boy behind him jumped and kicked the ball, but it continued to fly only straight up in the air.

The spectators followed the ball with their eyes. The ball disappeared from their sight and suddenly was on the ground.

Cheerleaders in blue skirts were enthusiastically cheering when the ASPARS made a score.

The ball was in the air and flew over Burak's head, and he was pointing his nose at it, directing it into the hands of a boy from his team. "Yes, it works," Burak made a sharp move with his elbow, supporting his words.

The boy hit it back, but the ball just stuck in the air. It was spinning in one spot then flew to Burak's head, bounced off him and hit Snick in his head, bounced again, and hit Gamut in his chest. Gamut took the ball in his hands because it didn't fall on the ground as it supposed to. His big lips separated because his jaw dropped in disbelieve.

Nobody saw what Burak was witnessing. The spectators saw as the boy from the BURGAMS team sent the ball, and Gamut caught it.

Burak and Snick were rubbing the painful bumps on their heads.

The spectators were impatient. The cheerleaders filled the gap between their performances.

Burak grabbed the ball from Gamut's hands and sent it over the net. Suddenly, he saw it split and become two balls. One flew to the other side of the net, and the other one fell under his feet.

"What is going on? It's your entire fault, Master Crowell, none of your spells work."

He grabbed the ball and sent it to the other side.

The ball multiplied many times and headed to the spectators. There was chaos in the stands as everybody was trying to get one.

The cheerleaders jumped higher than normal.

Mrs. Medusa's hair lost its clip, and she looked like the real Medusa, fighting for the ball, which Mr. Medusa was holding.

The players were screaming and hysterically laughing.

The loud blast from Dovry's whistle stopped the mess at once. Everybody froze on their spot and looked at each other, looking very stupid because only one ball was lying on the field next to the net.

I'm sorry, dear," Mr. Medusa said in a saintly voice, giving Mrs. Medusa the hair clip he picked up from under his foot.

"You broke it," she hit him with her fist, scratching his face with the sharp edge of broken clip. He felt guilty and didn't say anything to his wife.

With all this confusion, Dovry announced that there is no winner in this game. Most of the spectators left the stadium with some injuries and pain.

Double Vision

"What's wrong?" asked Snick sitting on Burak's bed. "Let me see your bump."

"Ah, get out of here," Burak waved Snick aside.

"You wanna see my bump?" Snick didn't give up.

"I think something is wrong with my eyes, or maybe I'm sick," Burak decided to share his problem with a sympathetic friend.

"What's wrong?"

"Everything is double in my eyes," His nose lowered until it was pointing at his knees.

"If you call that a problem, then I have the same problem."

"You do?"

"Ha, Rocco the Porpusales brothers double in my eyes all the time."

"Get out of here."

"The double is his twin brother, his name is Atony, and they are both weird,"

"Aaa," Burak rolled his tongue in his mouth. "The game was also weird with so many balls flying."

"You are, sick," Snick confirmed, moving farther away from Burak. "Where did you see many balls?"

"Uuh," Burak dropped his head on the pillow. Snick left his troubled friend alone.

I need glasses, Burak said to himself, and he went to see a doctor.

The doctor checked him and didn't find any problem with his eyes, but to make his patient feel better, he gave him reading glasses which just slightly magnified.

The small glasses fit very comfortably on his large nose. They were for reading only, but he decided to wear them all the time. "It's cool," he said to himself. He walked outside, and everything was very fuzzy. He imMedeately bumped into Gamut, who was sent by Snick to support the troubled friend.

"Uh, new glasses? Now you look smart in them," Gamut complimented him.

"You saying I wasn't looking smart before? Get out of my eyes," he walked ahead and Gamut followed him.

New glasses inspired him to use them.

"I'm gonna finish the letter to Master Crowell, wanna help?"

Gamut didn't have much desire to help with the letter, but it was not possible him to say no.

"Get Master Crowell's letter from under my bed," He gave an order to Gamut; he remembered throwing it there.

"Where is it? I don't see any letter here."

Burak looked under his bed, and it wasn't there. He nervously searched under every bed, and the letter was nowhere to be found.

"Oh," he sighed. "Trouble doesn't come alone," he shook his hands, walking to the window.

Through his glasses, everything was looking blurry, and he took them off, putting them on the window sill.

He rubbed the eyes with his fists and when he opened his eyes, a bird landed on the window sill and took off carrying his new glasses in its beak.

"Hey, give it back to me," he shouted.

The bird sat on the branch of a tree and looked at him with one black eye. Then, she stepped to the side of the branch, teasing Burak and flew away with his new glasses.

Burak even didn't have strength today to be angry. He sat on his bed and thought about the lost glasses, and Master Crowell's lost letter with the warning stamp of confidentiality and the multiple flying balls.

"The biggest problem," he sighed again, "is what to feed Mortelag."

Tired of failing at whatever he does, Burk said. "I need to recruit more people to help us to find the food."

"There will be a bunch of newcomers tomorrow," Gamut said, catching the dripping saliva from his open mouth. He took off the bandage from his injured finger. "I shouldn't have played the speedball, it hurts now even more," he muttered.

"You will live," said Burak, like always, making a comment to hurt people.

"Hey, what are you, doing here?" The black and white cat was swatting with his paw at the long strip of gauze bandage from Gamut's finger.

"Shoo," Burak didn't like black cats; he felt that there is something in them that he doesn't trust.

The Wild Ride with Aliens

It was the middle of the summer, and some kids were at the camp for only half of the season. The new arrivals will take their places. Also, new instructors are coming, and some of them will replace the old ones.

They were planning to give big goodbye party for those departing.

Aspar found his friends in the lobby and walked with them outside.

"Is there any good news, Aspar?" Atony asked, patting Aspar.

"They are going to recruit newcomers."

"Good, we will have fun with it," Richy said.

"That will be tomorrow. The fun will begin tonight," Deana added.

They went to the cafeteria area where announcements were pinned on the cork board.

'THE COSTUME PARTY"

"Great," Deana said. "I'm going to help the girls with their costumes," and then she ran to her house.

"What costume do you think will she wear?"

"I don't know, but she can change into many costumes if she wants to."

The boys were thinking of an interesting way to dress. All three of them decided to see what the other campers will be wearing because it was not a problem for them to create costumes for themselves in a short time.

At the center of the field was brought a big pile of wood with old dry branches. The tables, set outside, were bending from the abundance of food on them.

Campers dressed in costumes of pirates, sailors, warriors, and different costumes of animals. With Deana's help, the girls dressed as colorful birds, butterflies, bees and even flowers. Deana was dressed as a flower girl, wearing a wreath of flowers on her head.

The boys created costumes of magicians wearing capes.

Burak and his company showed up dressed as clowns walking on stilts.

The instructors, also dressed in costumes, organized different, but simple traditional games.

"Come with me," Richy said to his friends. Nobody saw them walking to the garden behind the building where vegetables and fruits were grown to feed the campers.

"What are you going to do with green beans?" Rocco asked seeing Richy collecting bean strings."

"You'll see. Help me to find the biggest beans."

Aspar was running around excited and followed the company to the field where the fire was already started.

Richy put the string beans on the grass and pulled out his crystal.

"I command you to grow to the size of a boat," he said waving his hands to the string of beans.

Instantly, they started to grow, and there were five of them on the field looking like rubber balloons with the beans protruded out of the skin.

"They are like camel's humps," Deana threw her flower wreath from her head and put on a hat with the large emblem of a Capitan, and the boys put on their Capitan's hats. They all changed into alien costumes.

"Who will ride on the fifth one?"

"Aaa, look at you," Atony said. "You out did yourself. And in this suit, you really look like an alien Capitan."

"I'm too light weight; this will give me stability."

"Ready?" Richy asked.

"Let's go," Aspar down on his Capitan's hat so he wouldn't lose it in the air.

"Your ears will hold it," Rocco said. "Don't worry."

Aspar wrapped his paws around the short stem and took off. He reduced the speed, waiting in the air, to let Richy lead.

"Zoom, zoom," one after the other, all five string beans were in the air.

"What is that?" the fingers were pointed at the sky. The sun was already down, and only the fire was providing light from the ground.

"Look, something strange flying in the sky," the campers were pointing and running after unknown objects. "Extraterrestrials are coming." Somebody shout.

"Ready?" Richy turned his head to Deana.

"Go for it," she shouted.

"Zoom," Richy quickly descended almost to the ground and grabbed Mrs. Medusa by her waist, placing her behind him.

"Uuh," Mrs. Medusa yelped and comfortably sat on the indent between the seeds under thick, but soft, fuzzy skin of the string bean.

The Capitan was looking like an alien and she couldn't even guess that it could be one of the campers. The alien abducted her. How she didn't know, but she wasn't scared at all.

Richy swooped down one more time and grabbed Mr. Medusa who took the seat behind his wife. Deana, Rocco, and Atony picked up rest of the staff and campers. Every string between the beans grew longer as more campers were picked up.

Burak, Gamut, and Snick, wearing their stilts as a part of a clown costume, couldn't understand what was happening. Aspar saw them as they left alone on the ground and he was after them.

Burak was running away when he saw a strange-faced alien storming toward him, but Aspar was faster.

In an instant, Gamut was picked by the big cat's paw and placed on a seat behind him. Aspar dove down two more times and picked up Burak, and then Snick.

Then he soared to the sky to reach the other string beans, and Gamut almost lost his seat.

"Hold on to me by my waist," Aspar shouted looking at Gamut with his glowing dark eyes.

"Oh, omnipotent, Golovorez," Burak exclaimed. "I doubted you, but you do exist."

The string beans, like long trains, were making big circles around the camp territory, dropping down to almost touch the fire and then soared up into the sky.

"Ooooh, Richy heard Mrs. Medusa scream behind him. He turned his head and saw Mrs. Medusa's long skirt from her costume, flew in the wind, covering her and Mr. Medusa's heads.

Mr. Medusa removed both of his hands from Mrs. Medusa's waist, fighting with her skirt to free his face. He floated into the air and was only holding onto the skirt. The snap holding the skirt broke and the skirt was stripped from Mrs. Medusa.

Feeling dazed, losing her skirt and left in her undergarment pantaloons, Mrs. Medusa looked down and saw as her dear husband was propelling downward with her skirt in his hands.

"Oh, my dear," she shrieked with the voice she couldn't recognize herself. "You are going to crash."

Richy was going to reach for the crystal in his pocket, but it was not easy to steer with one hand.

He looked for Deana and saw that only the girls dressed as flowers remained on the green bean. The girls in birds, butterflies and bee costumes were flying behind the bean on their own.

"Deana, quickly, do something or he will crash!" Richy yelled.

Deana saw Mr. Medusa falling and turned the skirt into a parachute.

"Oh," Richy sighed with relief. Mr. Medusa was safe and was smoothly descending downward.

Aspar lined up with Richy, and Richy saw that Gamut was in the air holding onto the stilts attached to Burak's legs, and Snick holding on Gamut's stilts. They were both flying in the air, stretched far behind the green bean. How long are they going last? Richy asked himself.

"I guess they had enough of excitement for tonight," Richy yelled to Deana when she lined up with him.

"I think they will remember it for a long time. Let's bring them home."

The green beans, one by one, landed on the grass, and Richy reduced them to the normal size. Even if they tried to find them, they couldn't, the beans shrunk to almost nothing and completely disappeared. Richy and his friends were back in their costumes of magicians.

Deana picked up the wreath made of flowers and crowned her head with it. She was dressed as a flower girl again as if she never changed. She winked with her eye and ran to her birds, butterflies, and bees, skipping and laughing.

"What happened, where did it go, was it real, or we are all dreaming?" All the instructors, adults, and kids, were on the field next to the fire running around laughing, screaming and shrieking. "What happened? Where are the aliens?"

"I must have been dreaming," said Dowry, who was standing next to Miss Maguey.

"I would think so myself if I wouldn't have witnessed....," she pointed at Mrs. Medusa in her pantaloons. Mr. Medusa was helping his wife put the skirt on her.

"By the way, did you see the missing boys?"

"No, maybe they were kidnapped by aliens," he laughed, walking away.

"Something is going on here," Ms. Maguey said to Sam who was passing by.

"What you mean the aliens?"

"No, haven't you notice that boys and girls are disappearing and nobody cares? I'm going to talk to Mrs. Medusa."

"Do you think she is capable of listening to you now?" He smiled with one corner of his mouth.

Miss Maguey walked alone to her house which she shared with the other young women working on the campus. "Somebody is not telling me the truth. Is it Dowry, or Sam or is the whole staff is involved in something mysterious?

Surprising New Campers

Nobody mentioned the absence of Avon, Hover, Stanislaw, or the missing girls the next morning when the departing campers took their seats on the train, and the newcomers were brought to the camp site.

Sam led the new group, and the old campers enthusiastically met them. A few trumpets were playing. There was a roar of clapping hands, and cheerleaders jumped like the corps de ballet. The remaining staff was greeting new instructors. The entire camp hummed like bees.

Richy, with his friends, were watching the procession passing with their cases of possessions.

"Holy Mackerel," Richy was surprised. "I can't believe it."

"What is it, Richy?" asked Deana.

"My friends Nicolas and Philip are here; I can't believe it. I didn't expect to see them here."

Richy ran to greet his friends and dragged them to introduce Rocco, Atony, and Deana.

Rocco stretched his hand to Nicolas, but Nicolas didn't respond and was looking at Richy.

"Say hello to my friend," Richy said to him.

"What friend?" Nicolas was confused.

"Philip, this is Atony."

"Who is Atony, where is he?" Philip wondered looking around.

They both were staring at Richy with confusion.

"Oh," Richy sighed, looking at Rocco and Atony. "My friends can't see you."

"They can't see us?" the brother's eyes became very wide.

"Who are you talking to, Richy?" Nicolas mumbled probing with his eyes.

"Can you see Deana?"

Nicolas and Philip were stunned. "Something is wrong here."

"Maybe our parents sent us to the wrong camp?" said Philip biting his lower lip.

"But Richy is here," Nicolas said not understanding what's happening.

"Maybe, it's not Richy, and he just looks like Richy?" They eyed him with suspicion and switched to a whisper.

"Can you see them?" Richy asked Deana, Rocco, and Atony.

"Don't be silly. Of course, we can see them."

Richy scratched his head, "We have a problem here."

"What problem?" All of them asked.

"You are not real," he said to the brothers.

"Not real?" the brothers exclaimed, "You must be joking, not real?"

Nicolas and Philip were peering at Richy who was talking to emptiness.

"If we are not real, how we can be real to everyone else, and we are talking to you after all?"

"Oh," Richy sat on Philip's case. "You are not real because I created you."

"Ha, Ha, Ha," both brothers chuckled. "Richy created us, Ha, Ha, Ha."

"Are you Richy Knight?" Nicolas asked lowering his voice peering in his eyes.

"Yes, of course, I'm Richy Knight," Richy said airily.

Rocco and Atony were puzzled with their existence. "What about Deana? Did you create her also?"

"No," Deana, said hastily, to avoid more confusion. "But I created the others."

"What others?" Richy jumped from Philip's case. "What are you talking about?"

Now Richy was puzzled, and he peered at Deana.

"The camp."

"The camp?" Richy's eyes widened to their max in astonishment. But he didn't have time to adjust to the overwhelming news as another unexpected thing took his attention.

"Do I see them, or I imagine them? Over there." Richy pointed at two boys struggling with their cases.

"Yes, they are real," Nicolas said. We saw them when they were getting on the train. Barbes' uncle Gotie, helped them to load the cases on the train.

"Oh, no," for the second time Richy sat down on Philip's case. "One thing is more fantastic than the other."

"What do you mean?" Rocco asked.

"Wait until Burak and Gamut sees Barbes and Godat."

"And what?"

"Burak and Gamut will go crazy," Richy slapped his cheeks with his hands. "It will be a big surprise for them because they are not real either."

"So, Burak and Gamut are not real like my brother and me because they were also invented by you?"

"You are right. They can't see Burak, Gamut, Rocco, and Atony."

"So, Nicolas and Philip can't see Burak, Gamut, Rocco, Atony," Snick said, "because he was lucky to have the gift to see imaginative things. No wonder he was a spy for Burak and Gamut and was often hanging around ASPARS."

"Uuh," my head is spinning," Philip said and violently shook his head to come to his senses.

"Oh, we will have fun here!" Deana clapped her hand when she could see the new arrivals, Barbes and Godat because they were identical to Burak and Gamut.

Deana skipped to her building, giggling all the way, in anticipation of explosive, surreal events.

"Let's be noble and help Barbes and Godat carry their cases to their room," Richy said to his five friends.

Barbes and Godat are Going Nuts

"Hey neighbor," Richy said with a friendly voice. "Let us help you with your cases."

Barbes looked at Richy and couldn't believe that he was seeing him here. He stretched his tiny lips, which sort of showed a smile. Godat's snubbed nose meet with his forehead and his eyes disappeared, and two large teeth were revealing a smile.

Godat said, "We knew that you left for some camp, but didn't know which one."

"His uncle Gotie came with money, and he decided to treat Barbes to a nice vacation. Barbes didn't want to go by himself, and that is how we got here," Godat explained everything very simple.

Gotie must have sold somebody special, like he once sold Margo to the guards, to come with a lot of money," Nicolas thought but didn't say anything.

"You all need to stop by the administrative building first to find out which room you will stay in," Richy said to the new arrivals and walked them to the tower building. In the administrative office, they were greeted by Mrs. Medusa.

The foxy expression left her face when she saw Burak and Gamut.

"What are you doing here?" her eyebrows moved together as she saw them in the line of newcomers.

Barbes didn't like the inhospitable hostess.

"We need a room," he said.

"You want another one?"

Barbes' lips made a full circle, expressing misunderstanding and he moved his nose at Richy, then on Nicolas, and back on Mrs. Medusa.

"Go to your room; you are holding up the line. Go, go." "Next, in line," she called.

Nicolas and Philip will replace the two departed boys in ASPARS room, and they were all happy.

Barbes was unhappy and was going to attack the table along with Mrs. Medusa, but Richy decided to take charge.

"Follow me," he said to the unhappy campers.

They went outside to pick up their heavy cases.

Nicolas and Philip were carrying their cases and Richy and Godat were helping Barbes. Three of them were carrying two cases, with Barbes in the middle.

There was one more case left on the ground, and Barbes thought there weren't enough hands to carry it now.

Rocco with Atony picked it up, and Barbes almost dropped the cases from his hands when he noticed his second case lift off from the ground and was moving in midair all by itself.

A shiver ran through Barbes' body when he saw it. But after the unpleasant greeting in the administrative office, he felt uncertain that he was at the right camp. He was turning his head from time to time to look over both shoulders to make sure that his case doesn't do something even more weird as it followed him hanging in the air.

Richy knew that two beds in the BURGANS room were vacant and he led the new arrivals to that room. The room was empty, the beds were made, and it was not possible to say which ones are available. Richy shrugged shoulders seeing Barbes' hesitation at what bed to take.

"Pick the one you like," he said, helping with the cases. "We better go now, so make yourself comfortable."

After choosing the beds, Barbes and Godat were starving, and the smell of food brought them to the cafeteria. It was already late afternoon, and the cafeteria was almost empty; only a few new arrivals were finishing their meals.

After the meal, they walked outside. Sam was staying for the second half of summer and was explaining the rules and activities in the camp to the new group, and Barbes with Godat joined them.

When Sam saw them in the group of new arrivals, he was surprised, what they didn't know after being in the camp for a half of summer, but didn't say anything.

The rest of the campers were busy playing and hanging around. It was a busy day for instructors as well.

"Aspar, what's the news?" Rocco patted his shiny black fur. Aspar rubbed his head on Rocco's feet.

"Oh, not much," he said, mischievously. "Burak and Gamut are in the forest hunting for porcupines. I think they got one."

"Really? That is good news."

"I saw two new instructors arrive this morning. When they talk, they make funny snorting sounds in their throats, and it reminds me of a domestic animal."

"Madam Claret is here?" Richy overheard the conversation.

"Uh huh," he said like he knew her. "With a match," he added.

"With Monsieur Perot?" Richy exclaimed. "Unbelievable. What are they going to do here?"

"Teachers need their vacation too and what's better for them than spending more time with their students," Aspar made a statement, squirming his back.

"You are right; they love students more than students love them."

Rocco and Atony never heard about the English and literature teachers from the Paris school because they were from the city of Sibul, first of all, and second, from the country of Medea.

Richy spent the evening with his friends Nicolas and Philip, showing them around. They found Rocco and Atony in their room talking to a new boy named Romy when it was time to go to bed.

Hey, guys, meet Romy our new roommate."

"Hello, Romy. We are glad you are joining ASPARS."

"Hey," the redhead with freckles on his cheeks and nose waving his hand.

It was too late to talk, and boys went directly to their beds.

Richy was touched by the soft wave of a dream as a piercing cry vaulted him, and he elevated on a foot over his mattress. With a jolting heart, he landed on the floor. All five roommates quickly jumped on their feet.

"Something horrible happened," Nicolas blurted worryingly.

In their pajamas with bare feet, they ran to the corridor.

The door to the BURGANS room burst open, and Barbes stormed out, shouting words nobody could understand in a howling voice. His bare white heels sparkled in the dim light of the corridor. Running after him was Snick, Godat, Kostas, and the new boy. Kostas tripped on his pajamas pants and slid a few feet on a floor. His pants were too long for his short and chubby figure. ASPARS saw as the other two boys from BURGANS room follow him.

The noise they made woke up everybody on the floor. Every door in the corridor opened, and scared faces followed the running boys.

Burak and Gamut vaulted from their beds after their doubles Barbes and Godat, choosing same beds, sat on them.

Running through the corridor, Godat looked back and saw as Kostas clumsily elevated from the floor and was flying in the air. He was holding his arms out like wings and his feet were dragging on the floor.

"Ooh, my Lord, save me! He is possessed!" Godat was shouting, running behind the corner to the staircase.

Kostas was squealing using fully his vocal cords, dangling with his legs and was painfully hitting Burak's and Gamut's legs. As a new arrival, Godat couldn't see Burak and Gamut, and he thought that some invisible creatures are carrying him to hell. It happened to them once when they stole the boxes from Richy.

Burak and Gamut were returning a favor to Kostas, and after they had enough of the pain, they dropped him on the floor.

"Aah," they ran as fast as their legs could carry them because the running crowd was going to knock them off their feet.

Kostas was motionless on the floor. The entire dormitory was in a panic. Not understanding what happened, all boys were pushing each other, tripping over Kostas and other boys on the middle of the floor. The doorways were jammed because everybody was in a panic trying to get through at the same time. Shouting, crying, screaming, they poured outside.

Richy spotted Barbes as he was gasping for air and walking in circles on the grass.

Barbes completely forgot that Richy was his enemy in school and at home.

"What happened in your room?" Richy asked trying to find Barbes' eyes which he kept closed.

"Ooh, you won't believe it," he was still gasping for air. "I was going to lie down on my bed, and it was t...t...t...there," he stammered and gave a tragic sob.

"What was there?"

"S...s...s...something invisible and it was alive." He looked vaguely at Richy and continued to walk in circles, terrified from horror.

"Ha, Ha, Ha," Richy stepped back laughing loudly. "Ha, Ha, Ha," he held his stomach howling with a laugh.

Barbes stopped and looked at Richy with a feeling of being fooled. He got red in his face and threw Richy a harsh glance. Richy noticed a couple of tears dripping down on Barbes cheeks. Richy stopped laughing feeling guilty. But nothing could calm down Barbes; he still was disturbed. He was screaming, 'It was alive. It was alive."

"You are overreacting," Richy was going to explain to Barbes, but it was impossible to talk because now the whole camp was on its feet, running in their pajamas, shouting very loud.

"The monster is in the dormitory, the monster!"

Richy saw that a long white gown was rushing between campers in pajamas. Mrs. Medusa with her tousled black hair, looking like the real Medusa, was running in a panic, yelling, "Mortelag escaped, Mortelag escaped."

Richy saw as Mr. Medusa caught Mrs. Medusa in his arms and sealed her mouth with his hand.

"Why are you shouting; you will reveal the biggest secret of many millenniums."

"Oh, my dear, my dear," she snapped with the knuckles on her hands in anxiety.

He hastily dragged her to the building and slammed the door.

Instructors and all adults were calming down traumatized campers.

Not far from hysterically, screaming Barbes and Godat were whirling like blustery bonkers.

"I'm multiplying!" Burak was screaming dazed because his "double" sat on him in his own bed.

Gamut ran after him blurting out, "Me too, me too, oh my, Lord."

"What happened?" said the breathless, bulbous boy from the BULBOX room running after them, bewildered by confusion.

"First were the multiple balls in my eyes," Burak was shouting, running and gasping the air, "and now I'm multiplying myself. Oh, my Lord, save me."

Gamut couldn't see anything in front of him, and he overtook the bulbous boy who couldn't keep up with them. Burak and Gamut stormed out screaming all the way toward a forest.

It took some time for the instructors to bring order and calm down the bustle because everybody now saw the doubles.

Richy feeling responsible for what happened asked Sam to find a new room for Barbes and Godat to sleep tonight. It was just impossible to explain why they need another room. "I'll try to explain it to him tomorrow," Richy said to himself, "or maybe not."

He saw Deana returning with other girls to their houses. He waved to her, "See you tomorrow."

Sam couldn't find Burak and Gamut. He came to the conclusion that they found a place to sleep somewhere.

Double Faced

The next morning in the cafeteria, Richy excused himself to Rocco and Atony, and asked Deana to join him at a table alone. "I need to talk to you before Burak and Gamut show up," and they found a small table where nobody could hear them.

"We will talk about disappearing campers later. Right now we need to do something with Burak and Gamut."

"It was so much fun yesterday," Deana giggled.

"Yes, it was fun, but if we don't do something with the 'doubles,' we are facing a problem. What do you think we can do?"

"You gave them faces; you change them," she said looking smart.

"But they are already here, and everybody saw the doubles."

"But not everybody saw all four of them together. You are the writer, and you can change whatever you want. Describe their faces to me, and I will do the rest."

"Brilliant idea, Deana," Richy exclaimed enthusiastically.

"Burak's nose will be smaller, ears shorter, and Gamut's forehead will be flatter. Ah, altogether, their faces will look softer."

"Are you finished?" she asked looking at Richy. He nodded, and she closed her eyes and made smooth waves with her hands.

It took her a few seconds, and she opened her eyes.

"Done," she said smiling.

"Let's join big table."

Philip and Nicolas were still confused about the invisible brothers.

"Is this chair taken?" Philip touched the seat before he sat on it.

The grass was sparkling in the morning sun when Burak and Gamut woke up and stretched their stiff bodies.

After sleeping under a tree in the forest, Burak must have got cold because his nose was stuffed up. He went to touch it with both fingers to make it breathe, and it was missing.

"Ah, ah, where is my nose?" he said, frantically groping it. "My nose is gone."

He pushed sleepy Gamut on his shoulder and jumped to his feet.

"You are not Gamut, where is he?" Burak shouted in a panic peering down, "Who are you?"

Gamut opened his eyes and blinked a few times.

"It's you, but your nose is gone," he was stunned.

"I recognize your ears," Burak said, "But you look better," he cackled.

"Yeah, you look better too. Maybe sleeping in the forest will make you smarter too?"

"Don't start with me." Burak cut him short. "It was worth it to get a cold to reduce the size of my nose."

"I always thought that your nose is too big."

"Ah, shut up," Burak barked not pleased with the insulting comment.

"We need to eat; they must be finishing breakfast by now."

"I'm starving."

As they approached the cafeteria window, both of them peered into glass using it as a mirror to see their faces.

"Here they come," Deana said.

"Good job," Richy exclaimed.

As they chose food, they spotted Barbes and Godat.

"Uh, what a relief not to be double," Burak said stuffing his still small mouth with a blueberry muffin.

Barbes and Godat could care less how Burak and Gamut look because they couldn't see them anyway.

Madam Claret's Discovery

With the exception of Monsieur Perot, not many people knew that Madam Claret has a degree in the English language and a degree in history as well. She just adored hearing the stories about peoples and times in history.

When Mrs. Medusa found out about her passion, she was happy to have her as a friend and invited her for a cup of sweet tea at her apartment.

"Make yourself at home, my dear Madam Claret," Mrs. Medusa put teacups on the table. "Lately, so many strange things happening here, and I don't have a single soul to talk to about it, except my dear husband."

Madam Claret was very intrigued with 'many strange things.'

"And what are they, the strange things?"

Mrs. Medusa poured tea in Madam Claret's cup. She was hesitant to tell her, or not mention it at all. To give herself time to decide it, she touched Madam Claret's hair.

"Your hair must be very long to have it wrapped three times around your head."

"It's grown very fast since I cut it last winter. But what about the strange things, you mentioned?"

"Well, you see Madam Claret, this camp miraculously came to be only a few summers ago."

"Really, I thought that it has very old buildings."

"Maybe they look old, but they are new."

"I see," Madam Claret said, biting an oversweet and hard cookie.

"Do you like them? My husband is the cook here, but this is my recipe, and I baked them myself."

"They are fabulous," and Madam Claret soaked it in sweet tea.

"Sugar?" Mrs. Medusa was going to pass the large sugar container to Madam Claret.

"Thank you, dear, for the sugar. After this sweet tee, my system will have enough of it for the whole season. Now I'm all ears," and she confirmed her words by long snorting.

Mrs. Medusa nervously licked her lips and bravely said, "All this," she went over with her hands around the space, "is hanging in the air."

"Really, and what is under it."

Mrs. Medusa didn't have a choice now as to continue or not. She made herself more comfortable in her chair and whispered, "The ancient castle."

Madam Claret impatiently wiped her mouth with a napkin.

"More tea?"

"No, thank you, more about the castle please."

"I inherited the castle from my ancestors, and I lived there for many hundreds of years."

"Hundreds of years?"

"Many," Mrs. Medusa raised and dropped her brows.

Madam Claret watched her eyebrows and whispered, "I'm all ears."

"Have you ever hear about Black Magic?"

Now, Madam Claret's brows crawled up by themselves.

"Black Magic?" She snorted and caught the tea which was going to drop from the corner of her mouth before it came out.

"In good times, this region was a cradle of black magicians. They were produced and reproduced here to supply the world. The master, of all masters, who was defeated by White Magic, is still breathing."

The sound of snorting came out of Madam's throat when she noticed a black and white cat on a window sill. The window was closed, and she didn't notice when the cat came and jumped on the window sill, neither did Mrs. Medusa, notice he was sitting there.

"Shoo," Madam Medusa opened window and cat jumped out.

"We have our cat with a gray coat. I don't know how this one came to our camp. He is kind of weird."

"Mrs. Medusa, you were mentioning 'the things' earlier. What are they?"

"The multiplying balls, the snake in the toilet, the flying string beans with aliens, the walking case that doesn't have legs, all kinds of very strange things." She said, pouring more sweet tea for herself.

"This is all fascinating, Mrs. Medusa. I would like to see it myself."

"Ooh, don't' worry you will see plenty of it."

"I wish to see the castle. Is it possible?"

"Tonight," that is all Mrs. Medusa said, closing the window tightly.

"Thank you for the tea, Mrs. Medusa. I better go now to perform my duty and help Monsieur Perot lecture the campers, so they didn't forget what they learned during the last school year." She hurried out afraid that Mrs. Medusa will change her mind to show her the castle.

"Tonight!" Aspar said catching his breath. He found his friends in the stadium, watching campers practicing.

"What tonight?"

Tonight, two ladies are going to the castle."

"What castle?

"It's underground below the camp. Here she is coming," Aspar washed his face with his paw to look casual as any other cat in case she sees him again.

"Aaa, it is Madam Claret and Monsieur Perot," Richy saw them for the first time since they arrived. They stood for a while watching the running campers and walked out of the stadium.

"Mrs. Medusa is going to bring Madam Claret to the castle. "Are we going?"

"You bet," the ASPARS replied.

"Deana?" Aspar looked at her.

"I won't miss the fun," she scratched behind Aspar's ear.

"Purr, I better take a nap, the night will be long," Aspar skipped over the seats and left the stadium.

The Goldwiche's Party

Deana, dressed in a comfortable blue jumpsuit, was waiting outside for boys. The door opened, and the ASPARS, dressed in similar suits, very quickly walked out, heading to the tower building.

As they approached the entrance, Deana pulled Richy by the sleeve to hide. All of them stood in a deep shadow made by the column because the huge moon lit the earth too bright for their adventure.

"I hope all of you have your crystals with you."

"Don't worry, Deana. We never leave home without them."

Aspar came from nowhere and joined them.

"I almost missed...,"

"Shssh," Richy made him be quiet, "there they are."

Tiptoeing, half bent over, four figures were crossing the distance between Mr. and Mrs. Medusa's house and the tower building.

"Mr. and Mrs. Medusa, Madam Claret, and Monsieur Perot," Aspar named them.

They watched as Mr. Medusa opened the camouflaged door in the stones of the wall, and after thirty seconds, the ASPARS followed them and got inside.

They followed the light provided by an oil lamp that Mr. Medusa was holding in his hand. This time, he made a sharp turn to the right. The old wooden floor changed to stone, and the sound of their steps made less noise.

A sound like something was dropped on the stone floor, made them stop.

"Somebody is there," Richy whispered, pointing back.

They stood and listened for a while, but it was quiet, and they continued walking the long corridor that was descending downward.

"Oh," Atony called out when he was thrown to the side. The corridor was swinging like a bridge suspended in the air.

"Give me your hand," Rocco grabbed his falling brother.

There was a square light in front, and when they reached it, they were stunned.

Under the dark sky was a huge field of dark green grass or something that looks like grass. It was swaying though there was no breeze at all. The field was surrounded by a forest, or something that looked like a forest.

In the distance, there was an enormous gray colored castle or a fortress surrounded by tall walls and the castle had many rounded towers with tall pointy black roofs. Steam was rising from every peak.

As they approached it, walking on a sticky grass, they noticed that the pointed roofs had brims and they looked like witches hats.

As they walked, the grass became stickier, and it was hard to pull the foot from it.

Aspar spent all his energy to pull his paws from sticky grass, so he asked Rocco to pick him up. "Wake me up when you need me." He reduced himself to the size of a peanut and comfortably lay down in Rocco's pocket.

A deep ditch filled with water stopped them. The water was moving, like something alive was swimming in this dark water.

The bridge is over there," Atony pointed at the bridge which was hanging on thick chains.

"The gates are open, hurry up," Richy gave a command to the group. Invisible to Philip and Nicolas, the brothers followed them.

"Use your crystals now; nobody should see us," Richy pulled Deana to the bridge. All five of them became invisible and successfully made it inside, just in the nick of time because the heavy gates closed by itself behind Rocco and Atony. Nobody saw them get in, and now nobody could see them at all, though they could see each other with the exception that Nicolas and Philip couldn't see Rocco and Atony.

Unnoticed, they crossed the front yard and walked through heavy doors which opened for them without them touching it.

Their eyes opened to a huge hall, many stories tall, surrounded by colonnade and arches. The hall had a gloomy atmosphere with a dark ceiling, or there was no ceiling at all, and only torches on the walls provided some light.

"It looks to me that the walls are swaying."

"Everything is moving, even the stone floor."

"Oops," Deana stopped.

"Hold on to me Deana," Richy whispered, let's move ahead.

"This is a creepy place," Nicolas wiped his face, "something is dripping from the ceiling."

"It's blood," Philip cried out, seeing the red mark smeared on Nicola's cheek.

"More drops of blood are falling. Where is it coming from?"

"Shoosh," Richy stopped them again. A wave of hot air surrounded them and then went away.

"I feel like I'm in the mouth of a giant monster; it's so creepy here," Philip muttered.

They passed the hall and approached a high arch. When they walked through the gate and stepped into a bigger room, they have to hold their ears from the noise. Music, drums, whistles, clicking, shouting voices, all mixed into a harsh, discordant mixture of sounds.

The noise was made by three hundred or more creatures, crowded on the floor, flying in the air, swinging on ropes from balcony to balcony. Some were climbing a ladder to nowhere. A few were hanging on a huge brass chandelier and swinging on it, screaming and laughing, then jumping high in the air and doing somersaults.

It was incredibly hot inside, and the heat was coming from a huge fireplace. The flame was so intense that it was melting the mantel.

"Welcome to the Golwiches party," somebody invisible said.

"Uh, who are you?" Nicolas shuddered from the unexpectedness, and at the same moment, he was being dragged by a scary creature in dark green and red with different color patches and trims; a nasty looking clown. The creature with three crooked teeth pulled him to the center of the crowd.

Richy stormed in after them, but he was pulled by the other another creature, hanging from the swinging chandelier. Richy tried to free himself and see the eyes of the creature, but there were no eyes. Instead, of eyes were two black dots above a long nose which became a spiral at the end.

The creature held him tight, but suddenly a witch with a green nose, dressed in a long black dress and a hat with a pointy top, separated them by flying between them on a rope. The long tale of the witches' skirt was flying with her and the creature, which was holding him by his jacket, lost his grip. Richy fell onto the hard floor hitting his head. He saw what looked like rainbow circles, overlapping each other, multiplying and gradually transformed into scary faces.

The strange laughing and crying faces with pointy ears sticking out were dressed weird clown's costumes. Some looking like different insects were changing into a kaleidoscope in front of Richy who was lying on the floor.

Suddenly, Mrs. and Mr. Medusa zoomed over him, hanging on the chandelier.

"Holy mackerel, is it true?" Richy blurted out.

Mr. Medusa grabbed Richy from the floor, and Richy barely had time to hold onto him. He was flying in the air and landed on one of the balconies where Romy was sitting at a rounded table with the new red headed boy from their room with a bunch of freckles on his face. He was sinking his teeth into a huge piece of dark chocolate cake. He wiped his mouth with a napkin sewn into his dark blue color t-shirt.

"Hey," he said, "it's sweet, want some?"

"No," Richy said in astonishment, "are you...?"

"And you...?" Romy asked a question instead of giving an answer, spitting out some chocolate cake.

"Can you see me? Richy was surprised because he was supposed to be invisible.

"What, do you think you are invisible?"

That was the answer to his question.

"Get them, get them," Romy shouted, jumping from his seat. Richy looked in the same direction and saw as Stanislaw and Avon were chasing after Philip and Nicolas on the third story balcony. Richy grabbed the rope from a brown spotted orange creature with antennas on his head, which just landed next to him and flew to the third level balcony. But somebody already caught Avon by his wide pants and the pants were hanging empty in his hand. Richy watched as he threw them over the rail. He ran after Stanislaw and almost grabbed him, but Stanislaw spread huge violet wings and dove from the balcony down to the floor. Richy saw as his wings fold up, and he lost him the wild crowd.

"Look at these wings," a creature with green stripes shouted, "and he is from new Golvers. I heard that a new little Witch is in the harem."

"Do you know her name?"

"Oh, you have enough 'purples,' you 'bloodsucker.'" The creature squelched with his nose and dove downward.

Richy ran to Nicolas and Philip; they were gasping for air.

"Oh, you saved us, thanks."

"Don't mention it. What the friends are for? Did you see Deana?"

That same moment, he spotted her sitting at the big round table on the third story balcony in the company of Mrs. and Mr. Medusa, Madam Claret and Monsieur Perot.

"What is she doing there? Richy's heart gave him a jolt. "Is she...?" His forehead was soaked with sweat.

"Let's find Rocco and Atony and get out of here," Philip interrupted. "It's so hot here; it's bloody hell," wiping his wet face.

"Look," Nicolas pointed at a huge clock which was hanging between columns over the fireplace. "Are they going crazy, swinging on the hands of the clock?"

"They are not swinging; they are moving the hands backward," Richy said.

The hands got together on the moon, where number twelve supposed to be and the clock started banging. With the first bang, everyone froze in place. One by one, all creatures were sucked into the fireplace and vanished in the flame. Rocco and Atony grabbed ropes and jumped onto the floor. Richy, Nicolas, and Philip also descended on ropes.

"Get the peanut," Richy made a jaunty decision.

Rocco put the peanut in his palm.

"Aspar, wake up," Richy commanded.

Aspar jumped on the floor and yawned.

"Pump yourself up; we need a ride."

At the big round table, all five of them were talking and laughing as nothing was going on around them.

"Go get Deana and then pick us up; we are going home."

Aspar jumped to the third floor, grabbed Deana and put her on his back, then swooped to the floor, and all six of them on his back held each other tight. Aspar made his way between the abounded ropes and then flew out of castle through the open window. It was freezing cold up in the air after the extreme heat inside the castle.

Back at the camp, they dropped off Deana at her house, changed into their pajamas, and got under the blankets. Surprisingly they found Romy, sleeping peacefully in his bed.

The next morning when Richy opened his eyes, he saw Nicolas was in his bed, lying with his eyes open.

"Was it, or it wasn't?" he asked, looking at Richy.

"What?"

"The Golwiches party."

Richy noticed the sleeve of the blue jumpsuit sticking out from under Nicolas's bed. He lifted the sleeve, and there were blood drops all over it.

"It was real," he said in a gruff voice and coughed a few times.

"I can't think on an empty stomach." Nicolas said.

All boys were getting up, including Romy. Richy looked at him, and there was chocolate in the corners of his mouth.

"Let's go and eat something." He said not saying anything to Romy about last night.

In the cafeteria, they sat with Deana. Richy didn't know how to start.

"I know what you are thinking," she began. "You will be surprised what I found out last night."

"What?" Five pairs of eyes turned to her.

"They are using sugar to recruit new Golvers and Witches. The table last night was full of cakes, pies, custard, jelly, fudge, puddings, you name it, and everything was super sweet. The tea was impossible to drink, and they put more sugar in every cup."

"Did you drink any tea?"

"Oh," she laugh, "after I brushed my teeth a hundred times, I still have that bitter-sweet taste in my mouth."

"I know if you eat too much sugar, your teeth will rotten and fall out."

"Ha, Ha, Ha," she rolled her eyes, "not my teeth, Philip and after all, I didn't eat and didn't drink anything last night at that table. I was too busy telepathically transmitting a message to Madam Claret's and Monsieur Perot, the new victims of Golwiches."

Richy coughed clearing his throat, "It was so hot there, and after the ride in cold air, I must have caught a cold."

"Go and relax today, I'll take care of everything.

"Thanks, Deana," Richy left most of his food untouched. "I think I have a fever; I better lay down."

Rocco was feeding Aspar under the table taking breakfast sausages from Richy's plate.

Thanks' Rocco, I'm full now, I'll go check on Richy; maybe he needs an aspirin."

While Aspar was sleeping next to Richy's feet, Deana was slowly swinging on a swing, watching as Mrs. Medusa and Madam Claret walking arm under arm to Mrs. Medusa's house.

A girl with bright red tightly curled hair from CHIRAC'S house joined her on a swing.

"I don't know," she said, "whether I should tell Mrs. Medusa or not."

"What is it, Marsa?"

"Uuh," Marsa bit her lip, "one girl, from our room, Nadia, didn't sleep in her bed for two nights."

"Two nights and you didn't tell anyone?"

"We thought that she is staying in another house, but we found out today that another two girls didn't come back to sleep either."

"I'll go and tell...."

"Wait, Marsa," Deana stopped her because she noticed two ladies walk behind the tower. "Come with me." Deana got up from the swing, pulling Marsa with her. "Pretend that we are collecting these bluebells and follow me," Deana whispered, passing a group of boys loudly picking on each other.

Vibrating Town of Ghostbreed

Marsa promised, and Deana went to visit Richy.

She found him half lying on a large pillow on his bed.

"Feel better?"

"Oh, yeah, thanks. Aspar can heal anybody. He must have learned it from the Egyptians."

"With Aspirin?"

"No, he brought me some grass from the vegetable garden to chew. I threw up, and it helped right away."

"Good."

"You smell like an onion," Richy sniffed with his nose.

"I pulled the onion from the garden to use in the kitchen."

Richy looked at her with wonder.

"Listen, there is something more important to discuss," Deana looked at the door. "Three girls disappeared from the camp."

"Girls, when did it happen?"

"It started a few nights ago."

"They must have been recruited by the Golwiches and maybe they were at that party last night, but we didn't know that."

"Maybe, or maybe something worse."

"What do you mean worse? What can be worse than to be poisoned by sugar?"

"Oh, Deana shook her head, "there is no limit to a crime."

Richy's eyes opened wider.

Marsa didn't notice it, but I did."

"What?"

"Dovry was behind the bushes also."

"Dovry-the sport's instructor?"

"Uh huh," Deana nodded her head.

"Behind, what bushes?" Richy was confused.

"If you feel alright, we need to go," Deana said.

On the way to the garden, Deana explained what she saw.

"This bush, follow me," Deana headed first.

When they walked through the center of the bush which had a beaten path through it, they stepped into a different world.

Richy gapped at Deana. Her face had a lilac color. He looked at his hands, and they were lilac as well. The air was lilac and the trees, bushes, grass were the same color, only darker.

From the first step on the purple grass, they felt as if they were walking on glue; it was the same feeling as it was at the Golwiches castle. The grass, if it was possible to call it grass, moved all the time, it didn't have sharp edges, and it looked fuzzy.

A huge weeping willow with long branches touching the grass was blocking the view.

They pushed the branches aside, like they opened curtains and gasped.

"What town is this?" Richy exclaimed.

Under their feet was very unstable cobblestone. They looked around and everything was out of focus.

"What do that sign say?"

Deana squinted her eyes trying to focus.

"Kelleher's Laundromat," she read.

They crossed the street stepping on shaky ground.

Passing the Laundromat with mirror glass windows, they saw their reflections.

"Oh," Richy stepped back in astonishment, "we look like ghosts, but our skeletons are visible."

"You look awful," Richy said.

"Look at you," Deana poked her finger in Richy's chest, and her finger went through his ghostly body and touched his ribs.

"At least your skeleton is solid," she giggled.

Looking at the mirror, they saw that behind their ghostly images was life. Similar looking lilac ghosts were passing by and not paying any attention to them.

"They are not like us," Richy said.

When Deana focused her eyes a little better, she saw that inside the ghostly exteriors that looked human had skeletons of different animals.

"What is this place?" she pushed Richy with her body.

"Uh," Richy bumped into the muzzle of a prehistoric lizard.

"Watch where you are going, youngster," the creature said with discontent in his hoarse voice. He brushed his chest with the claws on his short fingers where Richy touched him and continued walking.

Their eyes adjusted to the lilac color and they could see the other colors.

"They are frogs," Deana whispered and pointed her head at two teenage frogs dressed in short skirts who were sauntering on their back legs. They were passed by a mother with a beak and skinny legs pushing a baby carriage with her wings.

"Excuse me," a filthy, skinny rat with pants hanging below his buttocks was storming through the crowd, pushing every creature aside, pressing a head of cheese to his chest with his hands. Wolves dressed in police uniforms with sticks in their hands were running after him. "Stop the shop lifter!" the police-wolf was shouting." Richy was pushed to the wall of a building and almost fell because the wall wasn't stable and it was dancing behind his back.

Deana pulled him, giving him a hand.

Richy looked at a sign hanging on a rusted metal rod over his head.

"The Muni's Café," he read the sign. The tables were set outside and waiters that looked like insects were skating on roller skates, serving drinks and sweets.

"Look who is sitting there," Deana stopped.

"I see a couple of herrings in silver dresses and an old turtle sitting alone, occupying two chairs."

"Look over there, behind the owl in glasses."

"Oh, no," Richy hid behind a goat couple that was kissing.

At a small table was Mrs. Medusa sitting with her legs crossed. Despite the hot weather, she was wearing orange fox coat. Her hair was a purple color and stylishly braided. Her puffy tail was resting on Madam Claret's hoofs, which were dressed in sparkling scarlet sandals with a stiletto heel. On Madam

Clarets' head was a scarlet color bow attached to her combed back and tied in big knot hair and she wore a sheer blouse with a green pleated skirt.

The tall, skinny lizard in a fancy dark brown suit, looking ghostly, quickly moved between the tables.

"Sorry I'm late," Dovry pulled out a chair and plopped down on it.

"Uuh, easy, easy, my friend," Mrs. Medusa exclaimed moving away form the table. Brushing her cup with his elbow, Dovry spilled the tea on her lap.

"Uh, thousands of pardons my dear. It was very clumsy of me."

"Waiter," Dovry called, "we have a little accident here, the tea spilled."

A grasshopper-waiter on roller skates rolled to them with a paper towel.

"What would you like to drink, your Viness?" he bowed.

"What is Viness," Richy asked Deana.

"I don't know; I guess he has some kind of a title and he is supposed to be addressed that way.

"He is a titled person, which is why Mrs. Medusa wasn't mad at him for making her coat wet."

"The pepperoni tea, please, make it double sweet," he added, "and double honeyberry turnovers for the ladies."

"Oh, you are such a gentleman," Madam Claret snorted.

"You are charming yourself Madam Claret, especially when you snort; it suits your pigginality so well."

The bleached eye lashes on Madam Claret's eyes blinked a few times from delight and soft snort followed.

"I never had such respect when I taught my students, they called me "Oink, Oink" it was so insulting."

"Oh, just opposite, Madam Claret, I love it so much that I'm going to call you 'Oink, Oink' myself."

"Ooooh, your Vines, I wouldn't permit anyone to call me like that, only you," and she forced herself to smile because it was bitter pill to swallow.

The triple sweet tea on Mrs. Medusa's fox coat dried and a big spot of fur stuck together, and it made Mrs. Medusa very upset, but she kept her wrenching out indignation inside.

"If you finished with your tea, Ladies, shall we visit our Institution of Convertality?"

"That would be lovely, Your Viness," Mrs. Medusa said with a false smile.

"Uuh," Madam Claret felt dizzy from over-sweetening herself and accidently stepped her stiletto on Mrs. Medusa's tail.

That was more then Mrs. Medusa could endure. She gave a squeak from excruciating pain, lurched forward, and without hesitation, slapped Madam Claret on her pink cheek making it scarlet red, which was a perfect color match to her bow and stiletto.

Madam Claret couldn't stand such disrespect. She pointed her hoof and punched Mrs. Medusa in her eye.

They charged toward each other. Mrs. Medusa's purple hair unbraided, her eyes become enormous, especially the black eye, and it made her look like the real Medusa.

A crowd of spectators surrounded the furious fighters.

Mrs. Medusa grabbed Madam Claret's scarlet bow and threw it in the air. It flew over the heads of the crowd and landed in Richy's hands. Richy quickly hid the scarlet bow in his pocket.

"Ladies, Ladies," His Viness stepped in to separate them, "you can put on a show in a theater, but, please, don't do it on the street."

"Where is my bow?" Madam Claret snarled at Mrs. Medusa. She was nervously rummaging between her ears.

Now both ladies were looking for the bow under the spectator's feet, but it vanished. Richy quickly wrapped the bow in his handkerchief so it would not be recognizable in his pocket.

"Oh, dear, your eye is bleeding."

"So is your cheek."

"Sorry, you lost your bow."

"Ah, rubbish, I didn't like it anyway," Madam Claret waved with her hoof.

His Viness was very pleased that peace was established and he took both ladies under their arms.

Richy and Deana followed them at a distance looking at store windows. They stopped for a moment at a bookstore window. On every book was written the words 'Black Magic' and then the title of the book. Richy took one book from the table outside of the store. It was being sold at a reduced price. "50% off," said a lizard with eyeglasses at the tip of his nose.

"Uh huh, Richy scanned the titles, 'Dictionary of Spells, 'Sacrificing Ceremonies,' 'The history of the Black Magia Empire' and countless brochures with recipes for potions.

"Richy we have to go," Deana pulled him from the table.

"My father has a bookstore, but the books are different."

"And not that old and dusty, I hope."

Richy thought about the magic book that he's still trying to find.

"You can't find it here, Richy," Deana read his mind.

'THE INSTITUTION of CONVERTALITY' read the sign on the building, carved in stone over the tall, massive wooden door.

Three skeletons with ghostly figures disappeared behind the door.

Richy said. "I hope we won't be stopped inside and asked what we are doing there."

Fortunately, a group of youngsters was walking inside, and Richy and Deana were able to mix in with the group. As they walked into the lobby, they were facing a wide black marble staircase. They saw that the Trio was almost at the top of the staircase and they rushed to follow them. Richy looked up, and there was huge stone on the wall with embossed letters, he read the slogan:

'LEARN, PERFORM AND PASS IT ON' - GOLOVOREZ

At the top of the stair case, the trio turned to the right and walked a long corridor with a ceiling that looked like bee honeycombs, but it was not bees that were flying around it. The dimly lit corridor was full of noisy black flies with green and purple florescent wings. They flew around Richy and Deana's heads and picked at their eyes. They put their hands over their mouths protected them from swallowing the annoying insects.

"Uuh," they both were shielding their faces with one hand and swinging the other in the air. They passed a few shallow recesses in the walls with suits of armor sprinkled with blood stains and reached the first door.

They noticed that the Trio just walked in. Through a crack in the door, they could see a laboratory. The sign on the door said 'Poisonotoria'. The tables were crowded with flasks, test tubes, and connecting tubs.

"The best equipped 'Poisonotoria' in the whole region," they heard the piping voice was repeating many times. The disgusting colored liquids were boiling and evaporating, spreading a suffocating smell.

The nauseating cloud was rising to the ceiling and reached them, filling their nostrils.

"I can't breathe," Deana pulled Richy.

They decided to leave the Trio to inhale the bilious poison. Still fighting with the flies, they looked in another door with the sign, 'Demonology'. It took their attention. They peeked behind the door.

"This hall looks like a theater, let's take a seat behind the students."

"They are dealing with malevolent spirits," Deana whispered. "They are experimenting with supernatural beings, the demons."

"Astaroth!" one character in a judge robe yelled from the stage. "You discoursed willingly on the subject of fall, still pretending that you should be exempt from the blame." The judge was holding stopwatch.

CLICK! "Exactly three seconds and the battle was over. I predicted that it wouldn't go on for long," the judge said his line in a dramatic voice.

Lucifer, with his followers, fell into hell; the rest were left in the air to tempt men.

The setting on the stage changed, and Lucifer was in hell collecting forces. He organized the government and divided the land between Kings of North, South, West and East. Under these mighty sovereigns, there were many noble devils, dukes, princes, marquises, counts, earls, knights, presidents, governors and bishops.

All the noble demons were checked by the judge-black magician, who performed a conjuring trick.

The Black Magician swung his wide sleeves in the air, and a few demons appeared. The Angel with white angelic wings was sitting in a fiery chariot. "This is a pretender, kill him," he gave the order to an executer.

He swung again, and the devil prince was riding on an infernal dragon with a whip in his hand. He had a lion head, goose feet, and hare's tail. Then he turned into a human form with the wings of a griffin on a fire-breathing dragon.

"Who is the judge," Richy whispered to Deana.

"The Satan, Golovorez, Deana whispered in his ear, "the dethroned monarch, and the chief of opposition."

"Ah," Richy covered his mouth, the Satan who is the opposition to your uncle, Lunar."

The students at the front of them must have heard him saying 'Lunar,' and they were turning their heads to see who dared to say this name.

"We better get out of here before they find out who we are."

The next door they came to had a sign that read, 'Preparatoria'.

Ghostly students of all sizes, short and tall skeletons, dressed in muddy-green robes and dark gray aprons with goggles covering the most of their faces, were diligently butchering bats. They were pulling out the organs with surgical gloves on their hands and putting them into jars with liquid. All walls up to the ceiling had shelves full of different size jars with floating organs inside.

"It's so dark inside, how can they see what they are doing?"

"That is a disgusting bloodbath, and we can't stay here for long without getting noticed," Deana whispered.

"I think that the girls and boys were recruited by sugar poisoning and brought here to study the black magic."

Suddenly, a deafening sound of multiple explosions cracked the air and the doors "Boom, Boom, Boom, slammed about walls.

A herd of galloping teenagers with ghostly images of all kind of animals poured out of each door and stormed out to the corridor and went down the black stairs to the outside.

Richy grabbed Deana's hand, and they ran together with the crowd out of this Institution of Convertality.

"What about the girls," Deana said.

"We have to come back another time to look for them. Honestly, I can't breathe here," Richy was taking a deep breath. "I rather chow on Aspar's grass and throw up than to smell that poisoned air inside."

They chose a different street and headed back. In the distance, they could hear a calling voice, "Crystallized delicious baby salamanders from a local swamp,"

An unbelievably ugly, ghostly alligator, with an apron over his enormous belly was shouting and waving with his hand, inviting pedestrians to his restaurant.

"Coated in powdered sugar, fresh snails, rotten rat's liver on sugar rock, and snake's eyes in heavy sugar syrup. Come inside and taste free samples."

A Little mouse with two missing front teeth was passing out flyers. Richy got one.

'Visit the best dentist in the town.'

'Experience the new method of knocking out teeth with a newly invented heavy duty hammer.'

"This is definitely something to consider for an individual who has too many teeth," Richy laughed.

"Oy," Deana covered her ears, "what is that awful sound?"

"And smell," He looked at Deana as she pulled at her face.

"Uuh, I have goosebumps," Richy's face twisted into a grimace, his whole body twitched and a shiver ran through it.

Around the corner was a slow moving procession. Six baboons were pulling the bier. Walking behind it was a music band. "That's supposed to be called music?"

Walking backward was a raccoon with a conductor's stick, smoothly moving his hands in the air.

In front of him, a jackal was walking, holding a fat squealing rat by the throat, performing solo. Behind them, the rest of the band produced sounds that made your blood clot.

Behind the jackal, walked an ancient animal, unknown to Richy, with blistering skin and fin on his back that also served as a tail. He wore a ruffled metal, old fashion laundry board, which was hanged by a rope over his long neck. He was holding a porcupine by both hands and rubbed it against the board making an excruciating squeak.

An armadillo was drumming on an opossum's fat belly at an incredible speed. The opossum was very pale as his belly became burgundy red from the beat.

Behind the band were six huge, healthy ants carrying a glass coffin with the dead vulture.

The familiar funeral music collected spectators.

"He died from poisoning," Richy heard behind his back.

"Really?"

"Poor vulture," the sympathetic voice said. "He accidently ate a fresh rabbit while it was still alive."

Behind them, a few hired coyotes-criers were walking. Their howl could be heard on the moon, and it tore souls apart. After them, the grieving relatives walked with their heads down. Their eyes were solid red, and big tears were dropping onto the cobblestones.

At the rear was a well-dressed skunk, appropriate for the funeral, in a black and white outfit. By tradition, he sprayed the air with a deadly, suffocating, strangling poison.

"If you could describe what a headache is, it would be this smell," Deana said, covering her nose.

A young goat, about one-year-old, sniffed the air, closing his eyes from the delightful fragrance. "It smells better than we produce, right Granny?" the youngster said.

"Yeh, he is a celebrity, they could afford the best skunk in the city to keep White Magi's spirits away from the black soul of Golver. I believe he is going directly to hell because his death was accidental." The old goat explained to the youngster, patting his thin yellowish-white beard.

Covering their mouths and noses, Richy and Deana rushed out of Ghostbreed.

Oh, I have a terrible headache."

"It smells like death itself."

"Look, the bush. I'm so glad." Deana let out a groan.

They ran through the bush and almost fainted when they stepped out from behind it.

"At last," dizzy from the fresh air, they rushed to see Aspar to get his remedies.

They went to their rooms to relax and get rid of the terrible headaches.

A Murder?

Gradually recovering, Richy thought about all the animal looking ghosts in Ghostbreed. Were they people before and became animals or were they animals from birth? Children, like the one-year-old goat, was already a goat at a young age. It means he was born as an animal. But how did it happen that Mrs. Medusa was looking like a fox, Madam Claret was a pig, and Vines Dovry was looking like a lizard when they were in that town? He was puzzled and needed to ask Deana. Drained from his previous cold and the dreadful experience in Ghostbreed, he stayed in his bed until dinner. Fortunately, all boys were outside, and he could relax in silence.

At dinner time, Richy and Deana met in cafeteria hall, and Richy asked the question that's been on his mind. Deana had the answer for everything.

"All mortals, as they call all regular people, have some personality which is reminiscent of different animals. Madam Claret, for example, she snorts like a pig, and her face reminds you of a pig. Or take the criers at the funeral, they cry like coyotes and look like coyotes. The characteristics of the person took the shape of an animal suitable to their personality and became visible in the Ghostbreed town."

She knew it or understood from observation, but it made sense.

Anyway, they decided to keep the secret about town to themselves for now and see how the things will develop.

The Porpusales brothers joined them at their table, and Nicolas with Philip took seats next to them. They watched how food was disappearing as soon it reached the brother's mouths. They still couldn't see them, but now they could hear them, Richy worked on it, using his knowledge in telepathy.

Rocco moved his chair closer to Richy.

"While you were sick in your bed, something bad happened," said Rocco, covering his mouth with a napkin to tone down the volume of his voice.

"And something strange is going on in the camp," added Atony animatedly.

"What do you mean something strange and what's happened that's bad?" Richy asked worryingly and tensely peering in Atony's eyes.

"One girl, Marsa is her name," he whispered, "was found dead a few hours ago."

Deana's spoon stopped frozen in midair.

"Marsa? She is from CHIRAC'S house. She is dead?"

"Sssh, nobody knows yet."

"Ah," Deana nervously bit her lips.

"What?" Richy gave a glance at her.

"She knew about the bush."

All four boys looked at her not understanding what the secret was that was not shared with them.

Deana's face darkened. "How do you know that she is dead?"

Because we watched as Mr. Medusa and Monsieur Perot were carrying her to Mr. Medusa's house."

"What makes you think that it's Marsa, it could be any girl?"

"Her red hair, you can see it from a distance, nobody else has hair like that. It must be Marsa," said Rocco without a doubt.

Deana moved her chair closer to the table.

"Tell us everything you know about it. This is crucial. Where did they find her?"

"In the vegetable garden," Atony whispered.

Deana almost choked on a piece of apple. With difficulty, she swallowed it without chewing.

Deana and Richy exchanged nervous looks. "This is not the place to talk about it. The BURGANS are watching us," Richy got up.

"Look who is hanging with them?" Nicolas said without moving his lips.

"The redhead with freckles," Deana gasped, and Richy responded with the question, "Romy, quite a surprise, what do they have in common?"

"After seeing Romy at Golwiches' party, I think we have a spy in our own yard," said Philip.

"It's dangerous to have a conversation here; anyone can be a spy," said Richy.

"You are right, let's go to our benches; there's so much to discuss," everybody agreed.

In the middle of an open area of a large field between structures, some campers moved benches, and now two of them were facing each other where they could talk and be not heard by spies. The benches were used by the BURGANS and the other groups of kids to talk in secret. Aspar was already sitting in the center between the benches. He was diligently licking his paws, washing his face after having nice dinner, consuming a pretty good portion of smoked duck.

"Hmmm," Richy put on his thinking hat.

"What did you say earlier, Rocco, about the only one in the whole camp with red hair? Did anyone notice that Romy has the same curly red color hair, and...?"

"And freckles," Deana added, "There's a very big resemblance."

"You want to say that they are brother and sister?"

"It's entirely possible," she nodded her head.

It was time to share with the group their discovery of the Ghostbreed town and how they got there.

"When we saw Mrs. Medusa, and Madam Claret use the pass which is camouflaged in the middle of a bush," Deana started. "We couldn't stay any longer in the garden, and we parted with Marsa. I promised to come back to her. I didn't want to involve more people in this risky business, and I didn't take her with me. So, I was too late to protect her," Deana dropped her head being disappointed in herself.

"What was the motive to kill Marsa?" Nicolas asked.

"Somebody else saw us in the garden and killed her, so she didn't give away the secret about the bush."

"Who could it be?" Atony and Rocco looked at each other. Richy noticed their blinking eyes. "They are who brought the news to us. Big conspiracy is going on in the camp, and you can lose your devoted friends in a blink of an eye. Are they...?" His heart gave him a painful jolt. "If it's so, I'm the one who created them, and I am responsible for their crime." "Uh," he shook his head to do away with the awful in his mind for now.

"Could it be Snick?" Nicolas guessed, scratching his head, "He spies for the BURAGANS."

"Or Romy, her own brother," Philip suggested.

"What about Mr. Medusa and his new body Monsieur Perot, they are the ones who carried the body," Deana guessed.

"So, they got Romy before we could introduce ourselves to him," Richy said disappointedly, going back to the first suspect.

"You guys have to be careful with what you say in your room," Deana said frowning, very much upset about Marsa's death.

"We definitely should," Richy said pensively, moving his eyes from Rocco to Atony.

Nobody noticed as Aspar disappeared, finished with his licking. He didn't waste his time guessing who and why he was hanging around Mr. and Mrs. Medusa's house. It was probability to find something there and just lay down under an open window as normal cats do.

"Monsieur Perot," he heard the polite voice of Mr. Medusa. "I can't abandon my duty in the kitchen. You stay here and watch to make sure that nobody sees anything until Mrs. Medusa returns.

"Return from where?" Monsieur Perot was thinking how long he has to stay with the dead body.

"She went to talk to Dovry in the gymnasium. I believe she will be back shortly."

"Is Madam Claret with her?"

"I believe so. They are inseparable after their fight in Ghostbreed. It brought them closer together," he cackled leaving the room and returned to the kitchen.

A gust of wind opened the window.

Suddenly, a desperate scream cut through the air.

"AAA! AAA!" Aspar jumped on the window sill. He saw that Monsieur Perot was rooted to the spot with quivering hands in the air.

"She is alive, he screamed in a panic, "She is alive."

The breeze from outside tickled Aspar's nose and made him sneeze, "Aaa... Aaa... Achoo!" he shook his head.

"Shoo," Monsieur Perot threw his hands at Aspar as he was the one who is responsible for the waking up the dead. The breeze was moving her skirt that was hanging over the bed.

"She is alive," he was shouting and ran away from the house.

Aspar could sense the death of the person long before the person dies, and he often was next to the departing person to offer comfort as they step into another world.

Aspar watched as the ghost was rising from the body of a red-headed girl. He saw it many times before when he lived in Egypt.

"When young Tutankhamen died, I wasn't with him to save him, or even to comfort him. But I'm here and don't like death. I command you, the spirit of Marsa, go back to her body and live there until her time comes." He said silently moving his lips.

Marsa's astral body slowly returned to her physical body, and she stretched herself as she was waking up from a deep sleep.

Aspar jumped on the ground and ran to the front of the house where Monsieur Perot was laying on the grass, petrified from the horror, and was assisted by Madam Claret and Mrs. Medusa who arrived just in time.

His shouting gathered a crowd of campers, but Mrs. Medusa assured them that Monsieur Perot is fine. He was just in the sun too long and had a small stroke. Sam was there with the campers, and he was going to help Monsieur Perot bringing him to Mrs. Medusa's house but ran up to Dovry and stopped him.

"I will appreciate it, Sam, if you get the spectators out of here. I will help Monsieur Perot," and he pulled him into a sitting position.

"I saw her moving and she scared me," Monsieur Perot said still shaking.

"She is dead, my dear friend and you don't need to upset yourself so much." Madam Claret snorted."

She was patting his bald head, which gradually became pinker, and her snort effectively worked on him.

"Dead people don't move, my dear."

"You shouldn't be left alone," Mrs. Medusa said sympathetically. "You are too sensitive and fragile."

They all walked Monsieur Perot to the house to give him a cup of cold sweet tea.

"Where is the body?" Monsieur Perot asked and then collapsed for the second time.

Stunningly, they peered at the empty bed.

"Where is the body?" bewildered, they spoke in one voice.

When Monsieur Perot was lying unconscious on the ground, Aspar ran to see his friends and rushed them to retrieve Marsa from the house. They used the open window, and Marsa was safely brought to the CHIRAC'S house. Deana explained to the girls that it was a misunderstanding and that Marsa was never lost in the first place. The girls were glad to hear it because Nadia, from their room, went missing for a long time and never came back.

Seeing that her friend was unconscious for the second time, Madam Claret remembered that cold water could stop any hysteric. It stopped her uncontrollable laughter. "It might work in this extreme situation," she thought.

Without hesitation, she rushed to the kitchen. Fortunately, Mr. Medusa brought a lot of ice from the kitchen fridge for the Marsa's body preservation and now the ice almost melted. Madam Claret grabbed the bucket with icy cold water and hurried to the living room where Monsieur Perot was motionless laying on the floor. She emptied the whole bucket on him.

Monsieur Perot sprang a good two feet from the floor and dropped back on the floor.

"What was that for?" he shouted nonplussed.

Feeling dazed, he was sitting in a puddle of water, splashing water on everyone as he moved his arms.

Madam Claret fell on her knees, begging for forgiveness.

This scene took all their attention, and they forgot about the missing body for a moment.

Mrs. Medusa brought Mr. Medusa's warm robe to replace Monsieur Perot's wet clothes, and they all walked him to his home because it was time to go to bed.

The Astral Cemetery

While Burak, Gamut, and the recruited, Barbes and Godat were busy with finding food for Mortelag, and hunting in the forest for porcupines because the one they caught somehow ran away, Richy and Deana took their friends to Ghostbreed. Richy felt guilty suspecting the two brothers in a crime they not committed. The good thing was that they didn't know about his suspicions. Nicolas and Philip have been through so much at home with him; it was time to show them something new and outrages.

"Is it sticky there?" Aspar asked. He wasn't interested much in the Ghostbreed town, and he asked Rocco to put him in his pocket after he reduced himself to the size of a peanut. "Take me with you just in case you get into trouble," he said. "A good breakfast makes me sleepy," he yawned, squirming in the fresh morning air.

After their own good breakfast, one by one, Deana and the ASPARS walked through the bush and stepped into the lilac world. Behind the weeping willow was the familiar Kelleher's Laundromat. They explained to their companions the things they knew, like the sticky grass, vibrating buildings, out of focus vision, lilac color and not the unstable ground. The boys were impressed with the ghostly animal figures with visible human skeletons.

"Uh, yummy, I like the burned sugar smell," Philip said. A delicious caramel smell tickled their nostrils when they passed a candy store.

"Do you want to see what smells so good?" Richy asked him.

"Yeah," Philip licked his lips.

The door to the store was open, and they walked inside.

Behind the counter, wearing a pink apron, a wild boar was standing with tasks on both sides of his mouth. Very skillfully, with two wooden flat spatulas, he was turning melted sugar on an open steel hot plate, adding pig's milk and a stinky, poison looking green garlic extract to the mass by small portions at a time.

The dirty-green extract and piggy milk sugar turned to a disgusting gray color. The shoppers were watching as he opened a jar with cockroaches and dumped them into the burning sugar.

Philip almost threw up when the boar handed him a burned sugar coated cockroach on a stick. The boar was peering at Philip and waiting for him to taste it and hear the approval.

Philip looked at a coyote-child next to him that was drooling with a desire to have it. Philip forced a smile on his face and gave it to the delightful child. Then he was the first one storming out of the store.

"Look who is walking on the other side of the street," Nicolas pulled Richy by the sleeve.

"Ah, there they are," he recognized Avon and Stanislaw, walking in a company of three girls. That must be the girls who disappeared from the camp earlier."

"Right, and one of them, Nadia, is from the CHAIRAC'S house where Marsa lives," said Deana. "They are carrying notebooks. They must be heading to The Institute of Convertality."

The what?" Nicolas asked.

"That is the Institute where they study to be black magicians. It was founded by Emperor Golovorez in a prehistoric time," Richy said with confidence.

"Since that time, they learn, perform, and pass it on by kidnapping and recruiting fresh souls," Deana added with anger.

"There," Richy said pointing across the street. "One more ghost, the redhead, Romy."

"I can't believe it, but he is definitely Marsa's brother. What a tragedy for the family to lose a child to the black magic,"

"Not one family in the world without flaw," Deana said pensively.

"That's the truth," Richy sighed. "They were intoxicated by sugar. It's so easy to get hooked on it."

"It's possible to unintoxicate them," Atony made up the word. Our father had a few patients, and he cleaned them up."

"That's right, they didn't become white magicians," Rocco picked up after his brother, "but they became clean to have a normal life after that."

"Oh," Philip exclaimed, "look whose faces on display in the photography studio; Mrs. Medusa and Madam Claret, unbelievable," he clapped his hands.

Atony huddled to Rocco. He saw something that made him uncomfortable. He noticed that Mrs. Medusa was jerking her head and her eyes were twinkling, and Madam Claret was giving him a lopsided smile.

"They must love their piggy, foxy faces to come to this town to have their photos taken," Rocco chuckled.

Next to the Photoshop was a sliding door with dirty glass. Ghostly creatures were walking in and out, carrying bags with groceries in their hands.

"Cermingdon's supermarket," Richy read the faded sign, which was swinging on one nail. "Looks like this will be the last public place because we are almost on the outskirt of the town.

"Shell we…?" he looked at Deana suggesting to get in.

"I can't imagine what is there," she threw a fastidious glance at him.

But even with her vivid imagination, she couldn't believe what she saw when they stepped into the stinky, crowded market with a lot of displays and signs. The huge prices were crossed out, and lower prices were written in larger numbers. Everything was on discount.

The salespeople were shouting loudly, enticing patrons to only buy their products.

Two female rats were fighting for a yellow tail viper, pulling it from each other, and the fattest one got the victory. She fell on her back, holding the viper in her hands. Must be her husband who helped her to get up on her feet. The one who lost in the fight was leaving the market, shouting bad words on the way out.

The butcher on a big wooden table was hammering a huge knife into the scalp of a wild boar. Another one, on a side, was already open and the female butcher was pulling out the brains, hurling it into a large bowl. A long line was forming to buy it.

Philip was looking at a crocodile's heads hanging over the counter with hungry teeth in its opened mouth and almost knocked over the barrel with sweet pickled eyeballs of unknown creatures. "Uh," he made a grimace of disgust on his face, and his stomach became queasy when he saw intestines from some creature in another barrel.

All of them held their noses when they passed the spoiled fish section. Rotten herrings were priced very high. The fins, heads, eyes, and dry fish skeletons were all were sold separately. There was no discount in the fish department.

Next to it was a section of tails. All kind of tails were on display in square containers behind the glass. It was hard to say what creature they belonged to, but the most obvious were gray rat tails with a little bit hair on it.

Then there was a huge section with sweets. There was sweet jelly made of snails, sugar coated worms, a huge variety of crystallized bugs and countless displays of ears and noses of all kinds, shapes, and sizes with powdered sugar on the top. The sales shackle was constantly shaking more powder over and repeating in a piping voice the same words, "The best selection of ears and noses in the town, buy now." His fur coat was completely white from sugar powder.

Walking through the section of sweets, they breathed enough sugar to hate it for the rest of their lives.

When they finally walked out of the market, they have to brush their clothes from sugar powder.

"I think you need to wash your hair because it is gray," Atony said to his brother.

"You too," said Rocco, tossing his hair with his hands to get the powdered sugar off.

"It's a disgusting and weird place," Nicolas had a revolted look on his face.

"Those rat tails..." Philip shook his hand squeamishly.

"Ugh," Deana jerked with her shoulders.

Constantly chatting and going unnoticing, the company walked outside of the town. All six of them stopped in front of an arch with the sign.

THE ASTRAL CEMETERY

"What in the world is this supposed to mean, The Astral Cemetery?" Nicolas said frowning.

Richy had an answer for everything since he was reading a lot and loved to share it with the others.

"Occultists have given the name to this subplane because this is where the astral bodies disintegrate and disappear after the soul leaves the astral plane, either to reincarnate or to move on to higher planes, such as a mental or those beyond." The boys didn't understand much, but it didn't matter who can understand death.

Richy hesitated to get in. Maybe his friends didn't have that feeling or were less sensitive, but Richy felt like somebody is there and he will be watched.

"Come on in," Nicolas walked through the arch. The six curious adventurers stepped in a different world. At first, they didn't see anything because it was pitch dark.

They stood for a while to adjust their eyes to the darkness. Then they could see that a lot of activity was ahead of them. The ghostly figures crowded the space. Some of them were just motionlessly sitting; some were walking or gliding over the vibrating ground. They could hear the noise made by many voices talking, crying, and screaming. The difference with the population in the Ghostbreed town and the ghostly figures here was that the skeleton of these ghosts wasn't visible.

"Uh, it's so chilly here," they all convulsed from the cold, slowly moving ahead.

Look, there's a post with arrows pointing, and it has seven signs. The Astral Shell, Sleeping regions," Richy read.

There were different kinds of activities, Intellectual activity, Heroic activity, mystical and religious activity and Astral Hell.

"Astral Hell," Philip exclaimed.

"This is the place you don't want to be," This is for sure," Philip's heart skipped.

But Richy gained his strength, and he said. "Hmm, where will we start? I think before we visit The Hell section to scare us to death, let's see what the Astral Shell is?" Richy always liked to lead the group.

He read a description of the place on a flat stone. "After the soul...," "This is not interesting," he said. "It's just a description of what happens right away after death."

"Sleeping regions," Rocco read.

"Aah, this is like a waiting room, they wait here to enter into ascribed places. It's a typical waiting area. Look at them," Nicolas said, "They are so bored being stuck here for a long time."

"They are just sitting there," Deana shook her head. "There is nothing worse in any world than to do nothing and just wait. I would hate it."

"Ouch," Philip bounced forward and recoiled back. A ghostly sheep dressed in a long white gown walked in front of him. The sheep had a funny apologetic look because it stepped on Philipp's foot.

Deana giggled. "What is it doing here?"

"The lost sheep," Richy grinned.

"Would you like to have a tour of our old cemetery? Baa," The sheep blinked with its thin white lashes. "You must be students from, Baa, the Institute of Convertality. A lot of students are coming here to study death. This will be, Baa, very educational for you."

"Yes, of course, it would be nice to be educated." Richy took charge, "We will follow you."

"I'm happy to see living souls. It's pretty boring here, Baa," sheep walked ahead of them and started the tour.

"On your right," it pointed to a busy place, "is the section of Intellectual activity, Baa. This is the place where the astral bodies of souls unable to achieve and complete an intellectual work, Baa, or a creative project while they were in the material world." The sheep made a long sentence in a pleasant voice. "This is my favorite section," it grinned.

Richy wouldn't call it favorable, though he didn't see much yet. He had a feeling that an unpleasant spirit is there with them. Though it was chilly, he felt extremely hot.

Deana noticed that Richy was looking around and didn't pay much attention to their guide, but the sheep went on.

"You must know that many of the works of art in literature, music, and painting are first created on the astral plane, Baa. When the soul reincarnates, it brings a project, which it was unable to complete in its previous existence into a manifestation from the material world."

"Aaa," Nicolas said. "That's where the talents are coming from."

"You are right if you believe what I'm saying."

"She must have been a professor of something when she was young," the brothers exchanged opinions.

"Is that Galileo sitting there with the globe in his hands," Richy pointed.

"Oh, yes, that's him, Galileo Galilee. He is the one who confirmed the theory of Copernicus and was so sure that the earth is round and rotating together with the other planets around the sun. When the church subjected him to an inquisition, accusing him of heresy, he stubbornly insisted on it. To avoid death, he was forced to renounce from his discoveries. Do you know what he said when they read him his accusation, and he was renounced?"

The sheep answered the question not waiting for the response, "His last words were, 'Still the earth is round, and it's rotating.' He is still waiting to be reincarnated, Baa, because he has more ideas about undiscovered planets in different galaxies," the sheep sighed.

Suddenly Richy stopped. "Who is that?" He asked in worrying voice pointing ahead of him.

"Which one?" Deana asked. "There are so many of them."

"The one with the double face. The right side of his face is a clown. He doesn't look like a real clown. There's something devilish in him, and the other side looks like the devil himself." Richy felt that this is the one who is watching him because the radiating heat from his eyes gave him a chill.

"This creature has many faces, but he is no danger here. He is too busy to watch that his talents didn't stick into a newborn to cultivate the talent." Deana said and addressed the sheep.

"And that man," she pointed to a man with a colorful bird quietly sitting with a bunch of brushes in his hands. Richy felt a little bit relaxed after Deana assured him there is no danger here and looked at the man.

"Oh, Baa, this is the genius, Leonardo da Vinci, Baa. He looks sad because he regrets that he didn't paint more pictures in his life, he was so good in it.

"Uh, what is that?" They shouted when a huge bird, or a machine made to look like a bird, flew over their heads, almost knocking them off their feet.

"That is one of his inventions. He was dreaming of flying and came up with this idea."

"Geniuses are not born too often," said Richy.

"Baa, he will sit for a long time till another one like him will be born so he can accomplish all his plans, Baa."

"Oh, boy," Atony sighed. "Look at the left field; it's a war zone."

On one side of the field, Vikings in their armor and long spears in their hands were galloping on their horses. The sharp metal knives twinkled in the air, attacking the enemies. Some of them already lost their heads, but were still holding on in their saddles.

"I don't see them fighting in the golden-roofed hall of Valhalla among the gods," Deana sighted. "Men are always fighting."

The Roman's, wearing helmets with floating red hair, were galloping with sabers, cutting heads off. They were fighting to the death. The new Roman army was marching to replace the fallen. The defended the army of Napoleon when it was returning from Russia, and dying soldiers were falling on the snow.

"That one, he is Aeneas," the sheep pointed to one young man. "He is trying to embrace his father, Anchises, who died in one of the battles. But you see that his hands are going through him; he doesn't understand yet that his father is just a spirit."

"He is crying, but it's too late, Baa," the sheep, Baaed.

"There are North American Indians shooting arrows at red uniformed soldiers. It is a massacre." Richy said.

"Baa," The sheep said airily. "All the heroes of mankind are continually reenacting their battles and victories on earth in the astral plane."

"Those souls," she pointed the crowd at the lake, "are drinking water to forget former lives and want to be born again.

At the beginning of the world was pure spirit, but humans become bound to life by love and fear. Only a few can rest afterlife quietly, waiting for the circle of time to be completed when they become pure spirit once more. Most of them hunger for the world again, Baa."

The sheep led them ahead, and they crossed another line.

"Now, you are stepping into the oldest part of the cemetery called Mystical and religious activity, Baa," it livened up because even it didn't like to be in the war zone. "Here, Baa, you can find all the mystics of great religious minds. They live in the cemetery, and they call it heaven," she giggled.

"And now is the last section, Baa, The Astral Hell," the old sheep pointed at the largest and the oldest portion of the cemetery.

"What a creepy place," Rocco said in disgust.

"This is the abode of criminals, murderers, dunkers, thefts, and the most depredated human souls," the old goat explained, "They arrive here from all over the world. They are simply spectators constantly being reminded of their past crimes. You are welcome to step inside, Baa," the old sheep invited them.

Before their eyes appeared the worse place other than the battlefield.

"I understand your disgust," the sheep said. "I'm just a guide here, Baa, and I got used to it.

The atmosphere here," it continued in lecturing voice, "is similar to the one which these souls lived while still encased in their human bodies. There are muggings, rapes, bank robberies, murders, and all sorts of heinous crimes being constantly reenacted in this region.

There, you see the famous mafia boss, Alafon, Baa, he killed people left and right. For a long time, the authorities couldn't get proof that he was guilty of any crime; he was a master of his business, Baa. Eventually, he was put in jail for not paying taxes and there he died. There he is. He got skinnier; he had a fat face before, and now his flair is gone. He will sit here forever to watch similar crimes and have his regrets."

They were watching as three bandits with masks on their faces were robbing a bank.

The bandits already killed all people inside, and when the police pointed guns at them, one criminal grabbed a man as a hostage and threatened to kill him if the police won't let them finish their bloody job.

He didn't wait and sliced the throat of a poor man. The other two were running toward him with money in a sack, but they didn't run far; the police fired, Bang, Bang, Bang, and killed all of them on the spot. The policemen that were also shot are here.

"Wow," Nicolas said, "I hope I will never see this again in my life; this is gruesome."

"Baa, even though they can't take part in this bloody orgies around them, these souls sometimes project themselves onto the material plane and try to entice men to commit crimes in order to feel a sense of, Baa, gratification."

"What will happen to these souls after the waiting period?" Richy asked an intelligent question.

"The constant exposure to its evil deeds either disgusts the soul, thus helping to raise itself above its misery, or it debases it farther. Those souls who can't rise above a level of impurity are then disintegrated and dissolved into the dark pool of negative forces, Baa."

"There are no animals in this astral cemetery," said Nicolas.

"You are right; animals better than humans because they kill only to eat."

Knowing what land they are in, Deana thought about their guide. She is definitely a lost sheep to be here.

Richy went back in his memory. The dark shadow they saw underground in Paris when they looked for Margo was that negative force. Now it became apparent to Richy that it could have taken over them if Lunar didn't come to rescue.

"How is everything tied together," he thought. "Now, Deana, his niece is my best friend." He got closer to Deana. "Let's get out of here," he whispered in her ear.

"Thank you for the tour," they said to the old sheep and waved goodbye from a distance.

When they were far away from the Cemetery, Richy said, "Ah, I'm sorry we didn't ask if Golovorez was dead or alive; maybe his soul is sitting there and watching similar crimes."

"He is there, and you saw him, at the same time he is not there, but I know that he is still breathing," said Deana firmly.

"The double-faced creature was Golovorez?" Richy exclaimed with horror in his eye.

"Yes."

"How do you know?"

"When crime will stop all over the world, you will know that he is dead."

"That was a genius answer. I don't know how I didn't come up with it myself?"

"You are not a magician yet, you are only learning to be one," she got right to the point.

Tarantula's Trap

That night Richy couldn't sleep. His mind was disturbed by the images he saw at the astral cemetery. It was a very unpleasant trip, and he didn't like to walk on that unstable, constantly shaking ground. He thought about the more pleasant forest with green lives. He closed his eyes and took a deep breath.

"Ahh," Deana inhaled fresh air with her nose. "It smells so good."

"Finally, we can breathe after visiting the gloomy town and cemetery," Nicolas said pulling his nose. Philip was walking ahead, hitting the grass with a branch in his hand to make a pass because the grass became thicker with every step.

"Opps," Richy almost stepped on his heels.

"Why did you stop...?" Richy didn't finish his question. About ten feet in front of them was a door. It was almost invisible because it was camouflaged with vines.

"The door is not locked," Rocco whispered.

"We've been here before, and I didn't notice any door," Atony said looking scared. "Somebody is behind that tree. I just saw a strange looking face," he expressed in a terrifying voice.

The branches were swaying, but not from the wind, somebody was there. They got closer to each other, and fear ran through their mind.

"The door is open, hurry up," Richy said and ran to the door. He grabbed a rusty handle, swung it open and all of them got in. Richy was going to close the door, but it slammed by itself. He tried to push it back, but it didn't move.

"We are trapped," he said being suddenly horrified.

"We shouldn't have come here," Philip cried.

"We didn't have a choice," Nicolas said, "somebody was there."

"And that someone locked us here."

"Oh, stop it," Richy had enough of the quarreling. "If we can't go back, we have one choice but to go ahead." And he bravely stepped into a dimly lit space. There was light coming from somewhere, but it was hard to say because the space was evenly lit.

Their eyes were adjusting to the gloomy place. They were in a chamber with a high ceiling.

In the darkness of space, two bright dots were starring at them. The eyes were close to each other, and judging by the distance between them, it was possible to say that it is a big animal or another living thing.

"Ooh," One of the boys screamed in a choking voice.

Richy didn't have a chance to ask what was happening as he felt that something is holding him by his throat. At the same time, he hears the hoarse voices of others. Richy reached out with his hand trying to free himself and grabbed something shaggy.

"Deana," he shouted. Are you..."

Suddenly, he hears Deana's loud scream and the grip let him go.

His eyes adjusted to the darkness, and he stepped back in horror. In front of him was an enormous black tarantula. It slowly moved its fury legs. The boys were rubbing their necks.

"I recognize this tarantula. It's from the Theraphosidae family," Deana said.

"Oh, I'm so glad that we know what it called," Philip snarled, moving backward, "If it grabs us again, scream louder, please, I hate spiders."

"This spider is unusually big," Deana said, watching him moving up.

"Wait a minute," Richy exclaimed. "He is guarding something. I see a door."

He stepped forward and jumped back. There was a spider web.

"Uh, I'm glad that it's not sticky. We need to find something to break the web; it's so thick; like it's made of rope. He looked around and spotted a piece of rock.

"Atony, quick, hand me that sharp stone. Hurry, the spider is coming back. Rocco, find stones for you as well. We need to cut the net."

Richy swung his hand with the stone and boys did the same. The web broke and the spider couldn't reach them. It claimed higher, and the door was freed.

"We are lucky," Nicolas sighed, "that Deana knew how to scare the spider."

"Oh, right!" muttered Philip, still rubbing his neck. "It's easy for you to say, but I've had arachnophobia since I was a child."

"I'm sure the tarantula is guarding something. What do you think can be behind this door?" Richy asked Deana.

"I'm sure it's not a magic book," She said, teasing Richy.

"I agree with you, but what is this rustling noise?" He bent back. Something toppled over with a muffled sound next to his feet and moved away. Richy raised his head and gasped at the air. The ceiling was covered with bats. They were hanging up side down on roots of plants growing above the cave. Bah, bah, one after another, the bats were falling on them. In a panic, they bumped into each other and stepped on each other's feet.

"Yikes, I can't stand them. Richy, we need to get out of here!" Philip was shouting.

Richy, there is a key in the door, turn the key," Deana rushed to him.

Richy tried to turn the key, but it didn't move. The boys were shaking from the fear. "What to do, we can't get out, and the key doesn't work."

"Oh, stop whining," Deana snapped at him, "better help to turn it."

Nicolas rushed with a piece of root he broke off the wall.

"Oh, good," Richy exclaimed, "push it through the key ring.'

Using the piece of root as a linchpin, they were able to turn the key.

Richy slowly opened the door and closed it again.

"What, what's in there?" the boys were pushing each other, trying to get a glance at what is inside.

"It's raining in there," Richy said surprisingly.

"Raining, does that mean that this is the door out?"

"I don't know, but it's pretty heavy rain."

"It's better to be wet than to be trapped under ground with spiders and bats," Philip muttered.

"Do you want to go first?" Richy asked.

"No," I'm not that brave.

Richy used to take a lead and stepped forward.

"Aah," his voice was lost in the noise of falling water.

Richy thought that he is in waterfall and was trying to get air into his lungs, but to his surprise, he landed on something soft and dry. At the same moment, all his friends jumped out of water entirely dry. Richy tapped it with his foot and it felt like a rug. He looked ahead, "Where does it go? There was only one way to go, it's straight ahead." The walls in the chamber, if it was a chamber, didn't exist. They were a blurry, earthy color, the same as the rug under their feet. In a million years, they couldn't guess what this place was.

"Shoosh," Richy stopped the group. "Can you hear the noise?" He asked.

It was squeaking, clunking, scratching noises as only machines could make. Slowly walking further, they stepped into a tunnel with an arched ceiling which leads them to an empty, spacious hall.

"This is much better," Richy heard a familiar voice. "Much better when you are coming by yourself."

The tall, skinny Dovry appeared from nowhere.

"Mr. Dovry?" Richy stepped back.

"I know that you are visiting our world and have been present at Mortelag feeding, have been at the party in the Golwiches castle, visited the town of Ghostbreed, took a tour at the astral cemetery, and now made up your up to work in the sugar company. I'm very pleased that you have voluntarily come here to work." Dovry rubbed his hands in excitement.

"To work?" Richy blurted out, "to work where?"

"Let me show you," Dovry walked ahead. "I'll put you on an assembly line for now."

"Wait, wait a minute. First of all, we didn't volunteer to work anywhere."

But Mr. Dovry didn't hear him or didn't want to hear. He was walking between the lines of the conveyor, where boys and girls were packaging sugar.

"Oh, look, Richy, I recognize the two girls who disappeared from the camp, and we thought they are at the institution of Convertality, and Hover is here too. That is where they were recruited." Deana was following Richy and whispered on the way. "We need to get out of here as soon as possible."

"I hope everybody has their crystals with them. Ask Nicolas behind you, and he will ask Philip, Rocco, and Atony."

"The crystals didn't work in the Golwiches castle, remember?"

"Maybe it will work here; you never know in what devilish place you can step into during your life and you must have hope and to try." Deana gave a long, encouraging speech.

The answer came to Richy that they didn't have the crystals.

"This is where all six of you will work," Dovry said. "All you need to do is pour syrup in these cans with the living worms and seal it. The worms will crystallize, and in a few days, it's ready for the market."

"Deana, do something," Richy begged, "or I will throw up." The smell of worms with sugar dust in the air made him sick. He was on the edge of throwing up. He grabbed a can with worms from the conveyer and held it next to his mouth.

"Yeah," he spit right into the can with the worms.

It didn't skip Dovry's attention.

"Get out of here," he shouted pointing to the way they came. "This is unacceptable behavior. Only the marked ones have a reaction like this to our products." He was screaming and pushing them to leave the factory, like the boys were threatening to him, or to his poisonous factory.

Richy and the entire group were running as fast as they could and soon reached the waterfall.

"Leave this place at once," Dovry's voice followed them.

"Where do we go?" Richy didn't hesitate and threw himself into the water. The others followed him.

"Uh," he gasped the air. "Oh, good, you all here and all dry," He was gasping for more air. "Now run." And he floated through the door, like it wasn't solid, almost fell, tripping on a bat on the floor and ran through the last door. The group followed him.

"This was the worse experience I've ever had," Philip said. "We almost became victims of a labor camp."

“We have to thank Richy that he spit into the can with worms.” They could laugh now.

“We need to return to the camp before they notice our absence,” Deana said worryingly.

Dreams of Prophecy

On the middle of the night, Richy walked up and just lay on his bed with his eyes open. All boys were in a deep sleep. He thought about all experiences he had in this camp. "If everything in life was happening for some reason, what was my purpose to be here? This is not the place to find the magic book and the answers to my questions in life."

Not clear from where, but the answer jumped into his head.

"You can't ignore the evil because it exists and the best way to fight with it, it's to know its power. It is a part of knowledge because to fight the enemy you have to learn about them."

Kart from Atlantis said that I have a special birthmark and my sister, Margo, and Willy are marked as well, so we are chosen to fight the evil, and this is the purpose for us to be born. It will take many lives to conquer the evil, but it is a noble thing and it worth to live for," Richy concluded.

His attention attracted a black bird which was thumping its beak in the window. Richy just glanced at it and didn't like the bird; it was larger in size than the birds he sees every day outside. He went to the window to scare it away. But it continued pecking the glass with more force and Richy was afraid that it would break the glass.

The worst happened. The glass cracked and many small pieces fell out to the ground. The sound was loud, but nobody woke up. The hot air hit his face. An incredible power was pushing him to walk out of the window.

To his surprise, the ground was on the level of the window sill. He stepped out.

"Ouch!" He jumped on a spot. His feet felt the heat through the sole of his slippers. He looked down, and the ground was so dry that it cracked in the pattern of cobblestone. He wanted to go back, but when he turned around, the window was gone, and he was standing surrounded by endless dried land. Not a single tree or bush; not even single blade of grass was around.

Then he heard a squawking voice, "Come with me." He slowly turned, there was nobody around. The wings of the witchy black bird above his head made a rustling sound.

"Come with me," it flew ahead and stopped in the air, waiting for him. Not having any other choice, Richy made a few steps.

"Where are you taking me?"

The bird didn't say anything, and Richy made a few more steps. He didn't see anyone, but voices surrounded him. They were whispering, and Richy couldn't understand what was frightening him.

"Where are you taking me," he screamed.

"To the end of this field," the bird said.

"And what is at the end of this field?" Richy shouted louder.

"The end of your journey." The bird said squawking and continued flying.

Richy's heart was pumping erratically; the heat was so intense that Richy felt as if his insides were on fire, and he became very thirsty. He licked his dry lips, and they were as cracked as the dry land. He still has to walk, and couldn't understand why.

"Tell me, black bird, what is waiting for me there?"

"Not what, but who," the bird said.

Richy felt that his life is in danger because the place where he is going is not promising.

"Why I have to go there?" Richy didn't give up.

"Because you are marked," the bird gave a glance at him.

"Marked with what?" Suddenly he thought about his birthmark on the back of his head. He touched it, and it was cold as ice.

"That is for you to find out later," the bird squawked.

He felt that he had been walking for a long time and still there was no end to his journey. Soon, completely exhausted by heat and thirst, he was dragging his legs. His clothes got so dry that they started to rip and was hanging in pieces. The skin on his lips was hanging in pieces as well. He made his last step and fell. The ground was so hot that he couldn't bare it. He jolted and woke up.

"Uh," he sighed, being happy to find himself in his bed. "What a stupid dream," Richy wiped his perspired face with his pajamas sleeve. The bird in his dream was so ugly that it looked like an old sorceress. "What am I marked with?" Richy thought. There are no visible marks on my body or maybe I do, and I haven't discovered it. He opened the pajamas and examined his chest. He couldn't see much in the moonlight. He touched the back of his head, and nothing was there.

"It's just a dream," he thought. He remembered Kart, the old scientist in Atlantis, told him about a birthmark on the back of his brother's head, and that he and Margo have the same birthmarks. His birthmark is at the same place on the back of his head, and it's invisible because it is covered with hair. He touched his head again, but it was smooth under the hair.

He saw this dream somewhere in the middle of the night, and the rest of the night, he didn't go into a deep sleep and woke up a few times.

"There was only one person who could understand him and could provide some light on the mysterious dream; that is Deana." In the morning he couldn't wait to share his dream with her. They took a walk in the forest so that nobody could hear them.

Deana listened with strict attention, then she said, "Generally, the drought is an unfavorable omen in the dream, drought represent the absence of life."

This didn't comfort Richy at all.

"I don't want to think about drought anymore, but the bird."

"It wasn't a bird," Deana said.

"Then who was it?"

"It was a malevolent spirit, a supernatural being, and it was a messenger."

"A messenger from whom?" Richy's eyes widened. He was more scared now than in his dream.

"If the bird was looking like a sorceress, and it took you to the desert, it is a messenger from Golovorez."

"From Golovorez?" Richy shouted in astonishment. "But why I was taken to the desert?"

"Because Golovorez is the demon of fire and the desert is his residence."

"Looks like you know everything. Do you know how he looks?" Richy wanted to know.

"He usually wears two faces on one head." Deana looked at the scared to death Richy. "One face is very innocent looking and modest, but like creepy looking clown; the other face is the face of a real devil."

"We saw him in the astral cemetery, right?"

"Yes, he is like a chameleon who changes his color to match the surrounding. He can change faces, and he can transform himself into a demon of air, demon of earth, demon of water, or demon of subterranean depth. Sometimes, he appears like a shadow or, ghost. His faces are invisible, but his actions are devilish."

"Then I think I saw him a few times, of course not his faces, but his actions," Richy remembered the fire in Notre Dame and the dark shadow underground.

"Does he want to destroy me, and he is hunting for me?" Richy, fearing the worst, asked Deana.

"Yes, he is after everyone who is marked."

"Then my family is not safe; my sister Margo and my brother Willy, they also have marks. I need to go home. I can't stay here longer." Richy said panicking.

"But it's not the end of a season. One more week and we all go home." Deana tried to make Richy understand and to stop him.

"I will stay one more day and tomorrow night I am leaving."

The sound of a cracking branch reached their ears.

"Is somebody following us?" Deana stopped and listened. But they heard only the rustling leaves in the light breeze.

"On one of the hiking trips," Richy continued, "I remember there was a village and behind the bridge is a station where the train stops. It will be not wise to wait for the train at our station." Richy was thinking loud.

"I have nothing to do here," Deana said. "If you leave, then I'm going home too."

When he told his friend that he is going home, all of them suddenly got home sick. "We are going with you," they decided.

The next night, they packed their bags and, one by one, left the camp. It was a dark night, and nobody could see them leaving.

Deana was walking with Richy all the way. When they were passing the village, she said, "One more thing you have to know, Richy."

"What?"

"That I have the same mark as you."

"Honestly?" Richy said with surprise and disbelief.

"Yes, because we are related."

"We are? Richy shouted so loud that the boys turned their heads at them.

"Your grandfather from your mother side and my grandfather..."

A strong gust of wind took away her words. Deana would have fallen on her knees if Richy didn't give her a hand.

They passed the village and reached the bridge.

"Where is this strong wind coming from?" Richy screamed in Deana's ear. "Just a moment ago, it was so calm."

They were at the bridge now. Richy looked down, and the bridge was so high in the air that he couldn't see the river. The wind got stronger, and when they passed the tower, the bridge began to sway violently from side to side. Before they realized it, the tilt became so violent that they were thrown against the curb.

Around them, the wooden pavement was breaking with cracking sounds. They tried to hold hands, but the chain was broken. Philip was close to Nicolas, and he grabbed his hand, but Nicolas was thrown again before he could reach him and Nicolas began to slide from side to side of the roadway. Fortunately, one moment he was at Richy's leg and Richy grabbed him by his shirt and swung him back.

On their hands and knees most of the time, they crawled fifty meters or so, closer to another tower. The wind was so strong that it was hard to breathe. Richy's breath was coming in gasps. His knees were raw and bleeding. His hands were bruised and swollen from gripping the wooden curb and splinters piercing his skin.

Toward the last, they risked everything, rising on their feet and running a few meters at a time.

Looking back, Richy noticed that they weren't alone on the bridge. There were at list six more people trying to survive in the violent wind. One moment, he thought that he recognized Snick. Maybe it was Snick who followed us into the forest and found out that we were leaving, but who are the other people?

The violent gust of wind threw him against a curb, and he hit his head.

When Rocco, Atony, and Deana were on solid ground, they looked back, and they saw as the bridge as it collapsed with the rest of people plunging into the river.

"Richy, don't be afraid, you will be born again," Richy heard the last words of Deana. He looked up and saw her standing on the top of the cliff in a sparkling dress. He was already so far from her that she looked like a star in the dark universe.

"Deana Camrusera was his last thought, "the goddess of white magic. Will I see you again?"

In a split second, all his life flashed in front of him, and now he had more questions than answers.

"Where I am going? What was my purpose to be on the earth? Why was I chosen, and for what?"

He heard Lunar's deep voice answering all his questions at once.

"You are going to the astral dimension, but not for long because your mission on the earth is not complete. You were born to write your own book of magic and the story of your life because every born human has to do it. You were chosen to fight the evil on earth. You bravely fought your enemies, taught, and inspired the others to do it. For that, you deserve to live again. Use your experience from past life and bring more happiness and laughter to the humans. Write another magic book and you will be rewarded. I'll see you soon."

The wind suddenly stopped, and bright moon lit the ground. They looked down at the river, and it was peacefully carrying its waters like nothing happened. The bridge was gone, and there was no debris in the water. All three of them set on the grass and buried their heads into their knees in shock. How long they set like this, they didn't know, but when they raised their heads, the bridge was hanging over the river as if nothing happened at all. How did it happen, was it true or are we imagining it?

The boys were nervously walking in circles, dropping their hands.

"Why Richy?" Rocco said.

"It would have been better if we were thrown into the river, than Richy," Atony said wiping the tears.

Deana recovered from the shock.

"Richy will never die," she said. He is alive and well with his parents right now."

That didn't make any sense because they saw the bridge collapsed with their own eyes. But it's better to believe Deana's words than to accept what they witnessed. They heard voices behind them. Burak and Gamut were looking at them.

Rocco put his hand into his pants pocket, and the peanut was there safely lying at the bottom.

"How many lives do you have, Aspar?" Rocco asked his friend with a smile.

Margo's Visit to Doctor Lunar

It was the last days of August in London, and the air outside was already cooling down. Doctor Lunar just closed the window after refreshing the air in the examining room as the doorbell announced the arrival of his old and new patient.

"Did you have a good vacation, Richy?" Doctor Lunar greeted his favorite patient. Mrs. Knight, good to see you," Doctor Lunar shook her hand.

"And this is your little sister, Margo." Doctor Lunar said smiling.

"I'm very pleased meeting you, Margo. Your brother told me many good things about you."

"Like what?" she didn't hesitate to ask.

"Oh, he told me that you are very smart, very curious, and like adventures."

Cold water in bottles was already on the table.

"I hope it there will be no fish, this time," Doctor Lunar thought. With my new patient from the same family, you have to be ready for anything unusual. And thanks, to the Lord, it was pure and crystal clean.

"Would you like some truffles?" he opened a colorful box and moved it to Margo. She took one and closed her eyes, tasting the raspberry flavored truffles which melted in her mouth.

"Richy?"Doctor Lunar glanced at Richy.

"Thank you very much, but I don't like sweets anymore," Richy said, and a shiver ran through his body.

Mrs. Knight's face expressed wonder, since when does Richy not like sweets?

"I understand," Doctor Lunar said.

"Hmm," Mrs. Knight thought. "Since when doesn't like sweets?" It looks like Doctor Lunar knows more about her son than his own mother.

She looked at the doctor, who was sitting quietly for at least a minute and didn't ask any questions or even move.

He bit his lower lip and his eyes were moving from Richy to Margo and back to Richy. Another thirty seconds passed, and the silence became uncomfortable.

"What is he thinking about?" Mrs. Knight was wondering.

The next moment, she saw Doctor Lunar starring at her.

She moved her eyes down and stretched the folds of her dress on her stomach. The printed flowers on her dress were moving, the rose bats started to open, and new leaves were unfolding right in front of her eyes.

"Oh," she dropped the dress and looked at Doctor Lunar to see if he noticed it. But Doctor Lunar was shaking his head as he was getting rid of something. Finally, he said, "Mrs. Knight your dress is..." he moved his eyebrows up and down a couple of times.

"Oh," she said, closing her eyes. She was glad that not only she noticed it. "It seems that I am alright," she thought.

When the flowers stopped overlapping each other, because there was no more room on her dress for them to unfold and multiply, Doctor Lunar finally started the session.

PICASA

"So little Margo," he began.

"I'm not little anymore, doctor. I'm nine now." She let him know, just like her brother did at their first session.

Mother smiled apologetically from her chair and said, "They are growing so fast these days; much faster than when we grew up."

"That is true," Doctor Lunar said. Mrs. Knight thought, "Is he reading my mind? I even didn't open my mouth."

"Apple blossoms. What a miracle - apple blossoms. I'll never forget them...."

Doctor Lunar bounced in his chair when he heard the high voice of Mrs. Knight singing the words of a song.

But when Doctor Lunar picked up the words and sang, "I won't count daaays in saaadness...," Mrs. Knight jumped onto her feet. "Is it me, or him, or both of us," she thought in a panic.

"Ha, Ha, Ha," she giggled like a little girl. "I'm always like this, singing," she clumsily explained her sudden behavior. "My kids, you know, they make me very happy." "That is why I'm here; both my children are out of this world," she silently added in her mind, and she sunk back into her armchair.

"I can't blame anyone or anything," Paul Lunar thought, "but every time I see Richy, I act like a loon. Is it me, or him, or both of us? It's must be me because the kids were behaving like nothing happened.

"Kha, kha," Doctor Lunar cleared his throat. "So, Margo, while Richy was out of town, how did you spend your summer vacation?"

"Hmm," Mrs. Knight thought. How does the doctor know that Richy was out of town? Neither of us had a chance to tell him about it."

"Weeelllll," Margo stretched the word. "There were some confrontations with Serpulina at the beginning of summer, but then I wasn't at home myself. I like to travel, you know, to see different places, and to see different things," she said casually, looking at the picture on the wall of a cat standing behind an easel as an artist painting.

Mrs. Knight moved her eyebrow. "What in the world is she saying? She was at home with me all summer."

"Tell me Margo where..., Doctor Lunar didn't finish his sentence as the picture on the wall become alive, and Margo was pulling him by hand.

They stepped over the frame into the theater and took the seats at the front. Not clear how, but Richy and Mrs. Knight was sitting behind them.

The show must have started some time ago, and the next participant is supposed to be called from the audience.

On the center of the stage, there was a table with a small easel along with the pallet of paints on it.

The best known for her talent of painting portraits of a tabby cat named Picasa, dressed in a light green painter's smock, was sitting at the edge of a stage. Then she pointed with his paw at Mrs. Knight to get her to the stage.

Mrs. Knight was surprised and shy to be chosen, but Margo encouraged her to get on the stage.

"Picasa chose you for your blue hat because it's bright and suits you very well."

Mrs. Knight sat on a chair next to the table and, Picasa, standing on her hind legs, applied her paw in blue paint. Then she makes a few strokes on canvas. Finished painting the blue hat, she dips her paw into a cream color paint. She presses her paws in a rubbing manner, makes a few small strokes, and then she is focusing on the white flower which Mrs. Knight has on her dress.

When Picasa finished with the flower, she turned around and bowed to the audience.

Mrs. Knight took the portrait from the easel and went back to her seat.

The next moment, all four of them were sitting on their chairs in Doctor Lunar's office, and Mrs. Knight was holding her portrait in her hands. The wet paint smelled fresh, and she almost dropped it on the floor and surprised when she saw that Picasa signed it.

Mrs. Knight looked at Doctor Lunar and her helpless look said. "You see Doctor, what I mean about my children?" But she said. "I have one more child at home. His name is Willy."

To be continued……

Book Three "PH-02"